The Pain Eater

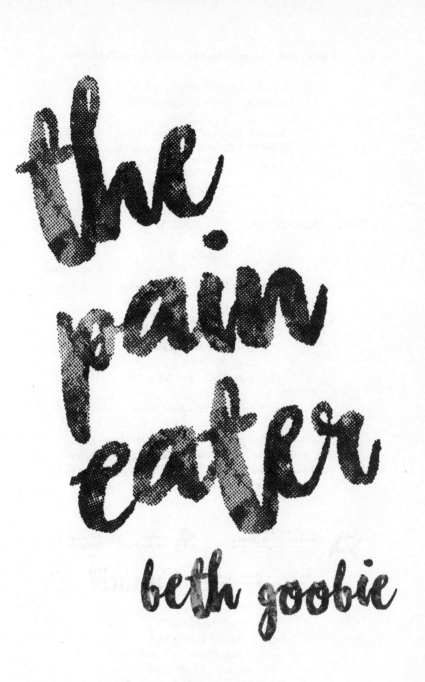

the pain eater

beth goobie

Second Story Press

Library and Archives Canada Cataloguing in Publication

Goobie, Beth, 1959-, author
The pain eater / by Beth Goobie.

Issued in print and electronic formats.
ISBN 978-1-77260-020-9 (paperback).--
ISBN 978-1-77260-021-6 (epub)

I. Title.

PS8563.O8326P35 2016   jC813'.54   C2016-903529-8

C2016-903530-1

Edited by Stephanie Fysh
Cover photo by Katherine Fellehner
Design by Melissa Kaita

First published in the USA in 2017

Printed and bound in Canada

*Second Story Press gratefully acknowledges the support of the
Ontario Arts Council and the Canada Council for the Arts for our
publishing program. We acknowledge the financial support of the
Government of Canada through the Canada Book Fund.*

ONTARIO ARTS COUNCIL
CONSEIL DES ARTS DE L'ONTARIO
an Ontario government agency
un organisme du gouvernement de l'Ontario

Canada Council   Conseil des Arts
for the Arts   du Canada

Funded by the Government of Canada
Financé par le gouvernement du Canada

Published by
SECOND STORY PRESS
20 Maud Street, Suite 401
Toronto, ON M5V 2M5
www.secondstorypress.ca

For the wounded ones.
When you are ready,
come back from The Beautiful Land.
We wait for you here, with love.

prologue

On a Thursday evening in late March, fourteen-year-old Maddy Malone was raped by three boys in a copse of aspen while coming home from a performance of *Our Town* at her high school. An additional two boys were present at the incident – one held her down by the shoulders as the others raped her, and the second stood an uneasy lookout at the edge of the copse. All five wore masks. They had also been at the play; in celebration of the cast's recent Best Production win at a regional high school drama festival, cheap plastic masks had been handed out at intermission, along with instructions to don them at the end of the performance as a surprise for the cast. The masks were simple white faces, half of them smiling and half of them grieving, in imitation of the traditional Greek comedy and tragedy masks. The five boys had been sitting together on the side of the auditorium where the smiling masks had been handed out; Maddy had been seated opposite, and so had received a mask of tragic proportions.

The copse wasn't on Maddy's regular route home; that night she'd walked a friend, Jennifer Ebinger, to her apartment before heading onward to her own house. Which meant the streets she was traversing were familiar but not overly so, as was the stand of aspen which grew at the edge of a park. Maddy had played in the park as a child; this late in the evening, however, the people she was used to seeing there – the dog-walkers and the joggers – had all gone home. So no one neutral was present to witness the event; neither were any phone pictures taken, or any live-action tweets posted by the lookout. Spur-of-the-moment, the act sucked up the boys' attention like a supernatural vortex, leaving no thought, no consciousness for anything but their own crazed heat until they found themselves running, still masked and hooting, down the avenue, away from the copse and the still, slender body lying among the aspen.

It was some time before Maddy moved. Her coat had been torn off, her shirt and bra shoved up, her jeans bunched down around her ankles. The night wind was bone-chilling cold. With one sharp movement, she jerked her coat over herself, then lay a while longer, shivering on the frozen ground. Finally she clambered, whimpering, to her feet, to find it took over a minute to get her jeans done up – her right hand had been twisted during the initial struggle, and she couldn't grasp the zipper properly. After buttoning her coat and pulling up her hood, she lingered within the trees, choking on tears and shaking so badly she had to press herself against an aspen to steady herself. Beyond the copse, both the park and the street were quiet – window curtains in the houses opposite were drawn, there were no pedestrians in sight, and only the odd car passed. When Maddy was certain no one was near – not even the dead out and about, lurking in the shadows – she untwisted the string around her neck and lifted the white-featured, weeping mask onto her face.

Shoulders hunched, she scuttled out of the trees and along the avenue, one of last fall's torn, muddy leaves blowing home.

chapter one

It was the following September, the first day of the school year, midafternoon. At the front of the second-floor classroom, Ms. Mousumi cleared her throat. Plump and middle-aged, with shoulder-length black hair and black-framed glasses, she looked the image of predictability. "Good afternoon," she said. "Welcome to grade ten English. This year, we'll be covering—"

Seated in the back row, Maddy huddled with her head down, listening. The desks in this classroom were arranged in two semi-circles that faced the whiteboard. The doorway stood at the back of the room; after passing through it, Maddy had made a beeline for the opposite wall, where she had parked her butt in the rear row desk closest to the front – out of Ms. Mousumi's line of sight, and hopefully everyone else's too. The girl who had sat down beside her probably wouldn't demand much in the way of idle chitchat – all Maddy knew of her was her first name, Kara, and her reputation for a quiet but remorseless braininess.

"This year's Shakespearean play will be *The Taming of the Shrew*," continued Ms. Mousumi. Scattered groans sounded and were reproved by the teacher's sharp glance. Head still ducked, Maddy stared at her hands. Methodically, every thirty or so seconds, the tip of her right thumbnail dug itself hard into a new spot on the back of her left hand. It was a habit she'd developed during the last months of grade nine – something that kept her mind focused and calm. Over the summer she'd laid off, but the habit had returned full force with the start of the fall semester, halfway through that morning's homeroom period. Now, ten minutes into the last class of the day, her left hand was covered with small reddening welts.

It didn't hurt, not much. No, if she wanted to, Maddy could give herself a real pain buzz, but she didn't need that. Not here. Not yet.

"This week," announced Ms. Mousumi, smiling brightly, "we'll be starting a collective writing project – a novel. Each of you will contribute a chapter of at least three hundred words. We'll go in alphabetical order, starting with…" The teacher paused to scan her attendance sheet. "…Kara Adovasio. Who is Kara?"

Beside Maddy, Kara raised her hand. Slender, with long brown hair and glasses, she looked as brainy as her reputation made her out to be.

"Ah – Kara. *You* will be our first contributor!" exclaimed Ms. Mousumi. "That means you get to decide what our class

novel will be about. Keep in mind that it has to be a situation
we can all write about, so nothing too specialized. Have your
chapter written for Wednesday's class, when you'll read it aloud
to the rest of us. Okay?"

Kara grimaced slightly, and nodded.

"Good!" Ms. Mousumi said brightly. "After you've read
us the novel's beginning, Kara, it'll be…" Again, the teacher
consulted her attendance sheet. "…Harvir Amin's task to come
up with the next chapter."

A definite groan erupted at the far side of the room, and
without thinking, Maddy glanced toward its source. Slumped
in his seat, a jockish boy was regarding Ms. Mousumi with
unmitigated dismay. "How many words?" he croaked.

"At least three hundred," said Ms. Mousumi, arching an
eyebrow. "That's around two pages, thereabouts."

"Two whole pages *full* of words?" demanded Harvir.
Sympathetic snickers rippled across the class.

"Jam packed with words," confirmed Ms. Mousumi. "I'm
sure you'll do a fabulous job, Harvir. This is your chance to
entertain us, to enliven our minds. Look at it as an *opportunity*.
You'll be reading your chapter of the novel to us on Friday
afternoon."

Harvir blinked, stupefied, and a mocking hand reached
out and patted his shoulder. Again without thinking, Maddy's
gaze followed that hand up to the face to which it belonged.
Her eyes widened, and for a moment she stopped breathing as
an invisible fist of shock rammed down her throat. Then her
gaze dropped, and she began once again gouging her thumbnail

into the back of her left hand. Panic thudded through her, giant footsteps slamming her chest. *No!* she thought frantically. *My god, no!* All last spring, through a seemingly endless April, May, and June, she had studiously avoided them. Of the five masked boys involved in the rape, she'd been able to work out the identities of three. To date, none of these three had been in any of her classes; she'd stayed away from anyplace they were known to hang out, and had gone straight home from school every day. Managed, she had managed, but now, here was one of them – Ken Soong, seated directly across the room. Skittish, Maddy's glance flitted across Ken's face. Grinning broadly, he appeared to be focused entirely on the now morose Harvir. Had Ken taken the time yet to scan the rest of the class? Had he noticed Maddy, hunched and skulking in her desk on the opposite side of the room? If not, he would soon – it was inevitable. And when Ken Soong's gaze finally settled upon her, Maddy knew she would feel it; she would light up like someone doused with kerosene and set on fire, her own personal nuclear holocaust.

• • •

Burrowed under her duvet, Maddy hugged herself and trembled. When the shakes came, the best thing to do – the *only* thing, she had found – was to hold herself as tightly as possible in order to keep the trembling body-sized. The other priority was to not think – it was of the utmost importance, no matter what, that she did not think. Because if she did, if Maddy let a single thought into her head, then memory would take over… and memory was exactly where she did not want to go.

Whether she wanted to or not, however, she was going there now. Back to the sound of sudden feet pounding up behind her, the voices ordering her into the trees. And when she'd resisted – when she'd tried, in fact, to take off, to run away – the hands that had grabbed and shoved her in among the aspen, away from the friendly light of street lamps and passing headlights. "Get her down, Soong," a voice had grunted; that was how she'd known Ken was involved – that, and his voice, when he'd spoken later on. By their voices, she'd also later been able to work out the identity of two of the other masked boys – Pete Gwirtzman and Robbie Nabigon, both one grade older and so unlikely to appear in her classes. But the names of the final two participants remained a mystery – a mystery Maddy didn't want to solve so much as to ignore, or, better yet, *disintegrate*…. Just give her some kind of magic wand, and she would wave it and make everything go away.

She hadn't told anyone. Not a single soul. Not one word about that night and what had been done to her had ever passed Maddy Malone's lips. She'd thought about it at first – had been desperate, even frantic, to tell – especially when her period had come late. But then her period had come, and her relief had been so great it had flattened her – left her lying motionless on her bed for hours, staring at the vast, off-white nothingness of the ceiling. There had been a rash that had lasted for a week, but Polysporin had solved that problem, and time had cleared the bruises. So even if she wanted to tell someone now, there wouldn't be any evidence, and without evidence, what was the point?

Maddy had followed news and Internet accounts about now-deceased Rehtaeh Parsons and her alleged attackers. The accounts were contradictory; some said the fifteen-year-old Rehtaeh consented to drunken sex with two male school peers; others stated she was gang-raped by four. What was incontestable was that one of the sex acts was photographed and posted online, followed by endless in-person and cyberbullying, which resulted in Rehtaeh's suicide. Of the boys involved in the incident, two received one year's probation each – both for child pornography charges. The police said there wasn't enough evidence to press charges for sexual assault. As Maddy recalled it, during the boys' trial the entire country was up in arms about the case; *everyone* was talking, in-person and online. Still, not one perpetrator had gone to jail – in spite of photographic evidence that *something* illegal had happened that night.

Maddy's family and close friends had all expressed indignation over the treatment Rehtaeh had received before her death; Maddy had little doubt they would believe and support *her*. But in the school halls and the cafeteria, she'd heard other points of view expressed – wisecracks and snide remarks about Rehtaeh's "wanting it"…and worse…that had left Maddy breathless with their cruelty – the kind of cruelty that was always waiting for the next victim to come along. In addition, there were no photographs of what had happened to her; Maddy had no evidence whatsoever. And with no evidence, she could just imagine the kind of gossip that would kick into gear if she went to the police. Every breath she took would go viral; every smile would be labeled slutty and come-on. That kind of nonstop harassment had killed Rehtaeh Parsons; Maddy had little faith she would survive it. As far as she could figure it, she would be out of her mind to come forward now about what had happened in March. She was just going to have to work out some way of ignoring Ken Soong's presence in English.

That wasn't going to be easy. Just seeing him, Robbie, or Pete in the halls could send a wave of acid panic through Maddy – she couldn't think then; she couldn't breathe, couldn't *breathe*. In those moments her body became a stranger, cringing into itself, turning and wanting to run – even if the boys hadn't seen her, even if they were walking away from her. It didn't seem to matter how many other kids were around, how much Maddy told herself this was here, this was now – whenever she saw Ken, Robbie, or Pete, she was back among the aspen, being shoved down onto the ground, into terror, into nothingness. That was what the rape had taught her, that was the truth she'd taken deep into herself: that without warning, without any possible way of knowing in advance, catastrophe could erupt out of complete ordinariness and be done directly to her. Anyone who thought otherwise simply didn't know yet; they hadn't been done to like that.

Under the duvet, Maddy's hoarse breaths came and went; her thoughts stuttered, stumbled, crashed. Her arms ached from holding on so tight; sometimes she left fingerprint bruises on herself. *Come on*, she thought, worn out from the inside of her head. *Get a grip, bozo. Get a grip.* Because, whether she liked it or not, she was going to have to figure out how to handle Ken's presence in English. Since the rape, he hadn't approached her in any way. Neither had Robbie. Pete had shadowed her in the halls for a while – just followed her around and stared, but he hadn't touched or spoken to her. Once, she'd found a picture taped to her locker – a blurred image of a woman who'd been tied up and gagged. Maddy had assumed the picture had come from Pete and that further threats would follow, but none had. In fact, that picture had been the end of it. Pete had stopped following her around then, and she'd never noticed anything else – not from him, Robbie, Ken, or the other unidentified two.

Maybe they were all as anxious to forget the incident as she was, Maddy thought, burrowing deeper into the duvet. The rape had seemed spontaneous; perhaps all five later regretted it. Who knew? As things stood now, it seemed almost as if some kind of a pact had been struck between herself and her assailants – an unspoken pact, to be sure, but still a kind of an agreement: If Maddy kept her mouth shut and let the memory die off in her mind – if she could act as if the whole thing had never happened – well, so could they. They weren't like the guys who'd photographed Rehtaeh then uploaded the graphic evidence of her humiliation onto the Internet. No, these five guys didn't seem to have even talked about what they'd done to anyone not directly involved. Other than Pete, Maddy had never noticed anyone smirking or looking at her knowingly.

Well, she thought, hugging herself through another long tremble, she couldn't drop English. It was a required subject. And Ken wasn't sitting *close* to her; he was way over on the opposite side of the room. So there was no reason they should ever have to speak to one another, or come into any kind of contact. In fact, Maddy didn't even have to see Ken, really. If she kept her head down and listened closely to Ms. Mousumi, she should be able to catch the gist of what was going on. And the whole time she was listening, she could pretend she was huddled in bed under her duvet like she was now – that no one else was around, it was just Ms. Mousumi's voice and her, and the teacher was nothing more than a figment of her imagination…not really there, not really there at all.

Then Maddy would have what she wanted more than anything. Even in a crowded room, Maddy Malone would be alone.

• • •

Wednesday afternoon found Maddy huddled, once again, at the far end of the back row. She'd arrived as early as possible, figuring Ken, one of the cool kids, would show up just before the bell, and she'd been correct – she'd known the instant he'd walked into the room, had lifted her head to see him standing beside his desk near the class entrance and looking right at her. Panic had roared through her; dropping her gaze, she'd clutched tightly at herself. By the time she'd been able to pull out of her terror, the class was underway, Ms. Mousumi talking about the unit on poetry they were about to start. A quick glance across the room showed Ken sitting with his head down, probably on his phone.

Yesterday, during Tuesday's class, he hadn't noticed her yet – Maddy was certain of this. She'd glanced at him regularly, every few minutes, and he'd looked calm and collected, joking with Harvir and David Janklow, the guy sitting on his other side. No way had he known she was there – *no way* – and maybe, Maddy had thought then, her heart lightening, he just wouldn't. The entire term would pass and his gaze would never settle upon her, huddled in the opposite corner of the room.

But today he'd spotted her right off. And it *had* bothered him: her presence had rippled his calm, cool exterior like the Loch Ness monster rising out of the depths. Just recalling Ken's intent expression now sent a wave of bile up Maddy's throat; she had to fight to keep herself from upchucking all over her desk. No way was she looking at the guy again, she thought fiercely. No matter what, she wasn't lifting her eyes….

"Kara, could you come to the front of the room and read the beginning of our class novel?" asked Ms. Mousumi.

Maddy felt the air shift as Kara rose and passed behind her en route to the front of the room. Eyes lowered, she didn't watch the other girl take up position before the whiteboard, didn't know if Kara read from a notebook or a tablet. The words, as Kara began to speak, came at first as if from a great distance – something mundane broadcasting from a radio, sound junk filling up space. But as the story progressed, Maddy began to tune in, and as she did, she felt herself coming into a stillness – not of boredom but of an interest so intense, it lit her like a stained glass window defined by light.

"This novel is called *The Pain Eater*," said Kara. "In the hills of Faraway, there lived a tribe that had a tradition. Once in each generation, they chose a child who had to carry the pain of everyone in the tribe. They called this child 'the pain eater.' At the time this story is happening, their pain eater was a fifteen-year-old girl named Farang. At birth, she was taken from her parents to live with the priestesses in the temple. The head priestess named Farang – it was the tribe's word for 'hunger.'

"Farang wasn't allowed to play with other children. She didn't learn the things women did in the tribe. She lived in the temple, but she wasn't taught how to be a priestess. She slept alone in a small hut, and spent most of her time wandering alone in the woods. If anyone from the tribe bumped into her by accident, they didn't talk to her. No one was friends with the pain eater; mostly people pretended she didn't exist.

"Except once a month, at the full moon. The full moon was when the tribe believed the heart was strongest, when it loved and hated and felt more than at any other time. At the full moon, the tribe held a ceremony in the middle of the night, where they danced and sang in the middle of their village. People were happy. They gave each other gifts. Young couples announced their engagements. This was a time of celebration, and everyone looked forward to it.

"Everyone, that is, except Farang. For at the end of the celebration, the tribe stopped singing and dancing. The high priestess walked to the middle of the crowd and raised her arms. 'Pain eater!' she cried. 'Where is the pain eater?'

"Then Farang came crawling out of the woods. She wasn't allowed to walk to the high priestess – she had to crawl, her face in the dirt, into the middle of the tribe. When she reached the priestess's feet, she had to wait there, crouched and silent. Everyone was silent. No one moved.

"'The pain eater comes,' the high priestess said, and shook her rattle. 'She comes to eat our pain, so we can be free of it. Don't worry where your pain comes from, or why – once the pain eater eats it, it's gone forever. Because when the pain eater eats our pain, it leaves us and goes into her. It's *her* pain then, not ours. That's the way things are. That's the way they've always been. That's the way they should be. So don't hold on to your pain – just give it to the pain eater. Then turn your back on her, so your pain can't come back to you.'

"All the people raised their arms and shouted with joy. Then, one by one, they walked up to the pain eater. They leaned down, opened their mouths, and pretended to spit something onto her. Some of them actually did spit on her.

"'Eat my pain,' they said. Or 'My pain is now your pain.' Over and over, they said this. Then they spat their pain onto Farang, turned their backs, and walked away.

"Then there was only the high priestess left. 'Pain eater,' she said. 'Eat my pain. Now it's yours and I am free. You are not me. You are not any one of us.' She turned her back, walked to a cage, and opened it. Everyone watched as Farang crawled into the cage and over to a bowl of food. The priestess locked the cage and Farang began to eat. Nearby, the tribe began to dance and sing again. But they also watched Farang eat. And when Farang began to shudder, they danced quicker. When Farang fell to the ground and writhed, they cheered and sang louder. They didn't know the high priestess had mixed a mild poison (the juice of the allura leaf) with Farang's food – enough to make her ill, but not to kill her. All they knew was that Farang had taken their pain and was feeling it so they didn't have to. As long as Farang suffered, none of them would get sick, or hurt in an accident, or die young.

"That was what they believed, this tribe who lived in the hills of Faraway. And every full moon until she was fifteen, Farang ate their pain and believed it too."

A brief pause followed the end of Kara's reading. Head still bowed, Maddy sat pressing her right thumbnail into the back of her left hand. "Well, that's it," said Kara, her voice for the first time uncertain. "Uh…do you want a copy of it, Ms. Mousumi? I printed an extra one."

"Oh, yes!" said the teacher. "I'd like to compile the individual contributions in a binder so they can be read by everyone. And I'd like to create an electronic version too. Can you email it to me?"

"Sure," said Kara.

"Tell me," said Ms. Mousumi, her voice growing thoughtful. "What was your inspiration for this story, Kara? Have you read Shirley Jackson's short story 'The Lottery'?"

"No," said Kara. "My story is sort of like 'The Ones Who Walk Away from Omelas' by Ursula Le Guin, but not really. It's way different, actually."

"I don't know that one," said Ms. Mousumi. "But I think you've given us an excellent start to our class novel. Thank you, Kara. You can sit down now. Well, class – any response? Yes, Julie?"

Kara sat down next to Maddy, as at the back of the room, from the seat on the other side of David Janklow, a girl named

Julie Armstrong spoke up. "This is, like, ancient times – before electricity and cars and democracy, right?"

"Yes," said Kara.

"*Duh*, Julie," said Ken Soong.

"Well, how ancient?" asked Julie, ignoring him. "Is it before the wheel? Before they invented agriculture and farming, and all that? I need to know – I'm right after Harvir."

Kara hesitated. "I only get to write the first chapter," she said. "I guess that's up to Harvir, really."

"Oh, Haaaarviiir!" came a mocking voice as Harvir grimaced.

"Enough of that!" Ms. Mousumi cut in. "This class will show respect at all times, or it will learn it in detention after the bell goes. Understood?"

A thoroughly understanding silence engulfed the room. "All right," said Ms. Mousumi, mollified. "Any other questions for Kara?"

Hunched over her throbbing left hand, Maddy's entire body was a question mark – a silent, unspeaking one.

"Okay, class," said Ms. Mousumi, when no one else spoke up. "I want you to open your books to page…."

chapter two

Back to the tree house wall, Maddy sat watching the lit cigarette between her fingers. The ember at its tip flared and ebbed, the red glow shifting within itself like a secret – a secret alive and flicker-dancing, so tiny most people never noticed it. And yet that tiny red glow had power – power that could take away what was wrong and make everything right. *Make everything right*, thought Maddy, trancing herself out on the secret red glow. *Everything right, everything right.*

Outside the tree house, the afternoon breeze tussled with poplar leaves. The tree house hadn't been built in one of the backyard poplars – they weren't sturdy enough to take its weight – but there were several nearby, and poplars were the trees the wind talked loudest to. You always knew when a poplar and the wind were having a chitchat, thought Maddy as she slid up the hem of her shorts. Talking back and forth about taking away the wrong – taking away the wrong and making it right.

Eyes drowsy but intent, she watched the cigarette ember move toward the skin of her inner left thigh. It was important to be respectful of this process, she'd learned – to honor the huge forces being tamed by the approach of fire to skin. There was fear, for instance, huge flames of it dancing inside her body; this had to be tamed, as did the pain that could explode through her flesh. But even in the beginning – even the very first time Maddy had brought living fire up to kiss her skin – she'd known she could do it. She had what was needed to tough out mind over matter. It was simply a matter of becoming all mind – of withdrawing in behind the eyes and watching what was happening to your body, but not feeling it. When you became the watcher, the body became something apart – something removed from you and entirely other, as far away as the cigarette ember that was now hovering like a tiny spaceship before a planet of flesh, about to make contact....

"Maddy!" called a voice, and the tree house vibrated as feet started up the outside ladder.

"Sssst!" hissed Maddy, and slid her shorts back down. Straightening her shoulders, she brought the cigarette to her lips and inhaled, just as her sister's head rose through the trap door opening.

"Hey, Maddikins!" Leanne grinned, her short blond hair a breeze-blown halo as she paused to survey her younger sister. "Thought I'd find you up here."

Still fighting off the tail end of her trance, Maddy silently held out her cigarette. Leanne took it and dragged, then settled down beside her. "Drawing?" she asked, her gaze skimming the tree house's interior. On all sides, chalk-drawn images filled the walls – sunflowers, the Taj Mahal, a family portrait Maddy had worked on for weeks last summer. In the latter, the resemblance between Maddy and her sister could immediately be seen – both blond and short-haired, gray-eyed, big-boned and solid-looking. *Trucker* was Leanne's nickname, but there wasn't an extra milligram on her, and she knew how to move on a volleyball or basketball court to devastating effect. Maddy, in contrast, was an average athlete. For her, it was color that called her name, as in *Maddy Scarlet, Maddy Mauve, Maddy in a Peach Pink dream.*

"Thinking about it," said Maddy.

"I ran into Mr. Zarro today," said Leanne, taking another drag. An occasional smoker only, she'd gone on a major guilt trip when she discovered Maddy had started smoking in grade eight. She'd cut her own smoking back to almost nil; to her dismay, Maddy hadn't followed suit. "He wanted to know why you didn't sign up for art this year."

"Grade ten art is next semester," said Maddy.

"No, it isn't, it's now," said Leanne. "I asked Mr. Zarro."

"Oh," said Maddy, taking back the cigarette.

"Come on, Maddikins – don't lie to me," said Leanne. "You know it's this semester."

"So?" said Maddy, staring at the floor.

"So he wants to know why you're not in his class," said Leanne, her voice blustering to cover her hurt. "So do I."

"I didn't feel like it," shrugged Maddy. The shrug was intentional – she knew how it bugged her sister. Two years older, Leanne had taken on baby Maddikins at birth as a life-long babysitting project; every now and then she had to be reminded to back off.

No, that wasn't fair, and Maddy knew it. There wasn't a better older sister than Leanne anywhere on the planet. Maddy was being a deliberate bitch, an unforgivable one.

"What's going on with you?" asked Leanne, the hurt now obvious in her voice. "This has been going on for months. Everyone's noticed – Mom and Dad, Aunt Cass. Even the neighbors. Mrs. Liu asked me about you the other day, why you always walk looking down at the ground. You don't hang around with your friends anymore. And you don't talk—"

"I talk," said Maddy, shifting away from her sister.

"Not like you used to," said Leanne. "Nothing's like it used to be with you. C'mon – why aren't you taking art?"

A grimace crossed Maddy's face. Silent, she stared at a chalk sunflower opposite, tracing its outline with her eyes. "Mr. Zarro's not the nice guy you think he is," she said finally.

"He gave you an A-plus!" cried Leanne.

"He was mean to some of the other kids," said Maddy. *Mean* was an understatement. For some reason, the teacher had taken a dislike to Jennifer Ebinger, a shy, quiet girl who'd sat next to Maddy in grade nine art. Maddy knew she'd never forget the way Mr. Zarro had stood, leaning over Jenn's shoulder and snapping, "Look at that line! D'you call that three-dimensional? What's the perspective on this – up, down, all around?" Rigid,

Jenn had sat, staring wordlessly forward as tears ran down her face, and Maddy had sat just as wordless beside her, horrified, wanting to intervene but not knowing how. Now she wished, more than anything, that she'd just put her arms around Jenn and hugged her – right in the middle of Mr. Zarro's heart-murdering tirades. That would've shown him *and* Jenn, she thought fiercely. Yeah, that was what she wished she'd done.

Instead, she and Jenn had never talked about it. They were still friends – Maddy was sitting directly behind Jenn this year in French – but to date neither had mentioned Jenn's repeated humiliations in art class. Jenn hadn't signed up for grade ten art, needless to say. But she didn't know Maddy hadn't either, or why.

"All they wanted to do was draw," said Maddy. "So they weren't Vincent Van Gogh. Since when is that a crime?"

Taking the cigarette from her, Leanne dragged, then butted it out in a tinfoil ashtray sitting on the floor. "Okay," she said. "He's a prick sometimes. But how are you helping those kids by not taking art yourself?"

"I can't draw for someone like that!" exploded Maddy.

"You did last year," said Leanne.

"I didn't know what he was like when I signed up," said Maddy. "I could hardly quit partway through the semester. But now I do know, it'd be like selling my soul to the devil, wouldn't it?"

Leanne's eyebrows hiked. "I guess," she sighed. "I just don't like to see you not taking art. You're happy when you're drawing. And you're good."

"It wouldn't be right," said Maddy, scowling at her runners but mollified nonetheless. "You make senior volleyball?"

"Tryouts are next week," said Leanne. "There's some tough competition, but I'll make it. I heard this fall's drama production is *The Merchant of Venice*. You going to paint the scenery like you did last year?"

Last year, the fall production had been *Bye Bye Birdie*. Maddy hadn't been involved with that play, but for *Our Town*, the spring production…. Her face twitched, and she shoved the memory away. "No," she said shortly, keeping her eyes down. Beside her, Leanne sat motionless, putting on the brakes, refusing to get angry, to react without thinking.

"Maddy, what's *wrong?*" she asked finally, her voice plaintive. All Leanne wanted to do – Maddy could feel it – was put her arms around her little sister's pain and hold it. Hold it until Maddy 'fessed up to what the problem was, and could be comforted.

But to tell meant to relive it. To relive every second of that heated, ugly, soul-shattering event. And Maddy simply couldn't do that. Last March, the rape had gutted her. It had reached into her, deeper than flesh, and pulled something out – the something that made her alive, that made her sing, dance, hope. She didn't know where that something had gone, only that it *had* gone. She didn't know how to get it back. What she did know was that since the rape, everything had changed. Colors were dim and shadowy; even the sun looked gray. Food tasted like cardboard. Nothing felt good; she didn't look forward to anything. Whatever it was that made life *alive*, the spark within all things, had gone away, and with it had gone what used to be her – the person Maddy Malone was supposed to be but was no longer.

Again, Maddy shrugged. Beside her, she felt her sister's hurt deepen.

Leanne took a careful breath. "You're not…doing meth?" she asked. "Speed…anything like that?"

Maddy snorted, then shook her head. Silent, Leanne sat a moment longer, her mouth working. When she spoke again, her voice had hardened. "Y'know, Maddy," she said. "Sometimes you can be a real bitch."

Crawling to the tree house entrance, she descended the ladder without glancing back.

• • •

Friday's English class loomed. Coming around a corner, Maddy saw the open door halfway down the corridor and was hit with a wave of nausea. It didn't get any easier – this was her fifth English class of the year, and still she was walking straight into sky-high panic as she approached that door. Just the thought of Ken Soong, of seeing him…. Again, nausea swept Maddy, stopping her dead in her tracks.

"Watch it!" said someone, clipping her from behind. It was David Janklow – blond, cool, and popular, and also the guy who sat beside Ken in class. As he passed Maddy, their eyes met; briefly his widened, and then he turned and disappeared through the doorway. Rooted to the spot, Maddy stood, bisecting the hallway stream of students as she worked up the nerve to approach the class entrance. Finally, she forced herself through it and into the classroom, where she made an immediate right, away from the direction of Ken's desk. Scurrying across the front of the room, she sank into her seat and concentrated on breathing – just getting enough air, sucking it in, gasping, *gasping* around the fist in her throat.

In front and to her right, desks filled as other students arrived. Kara took her seat without speaking; no one seemed to notice as terror gradually left Maddy and her body slumped. Soaked – she was soaked with sweat, her armpits disgusting. And now she was shivering, chilled to the bone.

A guy sitting directly in front of Maddy turned around in his seat. Tousle-haired and ruddy-faced, he'd been in several of her classes last year, but she'd never spoken to him. "What d'you figure Harvir's going to do to your story?" he asked, grinning at Kara.

Jeremy, thought Maddy. *Jeremy Dugger. Not one of the five.* His voice wasn't one of the ones that had been there that night.

Kara shrugged. "Axe it, probably," she said. "Turn it into something about hockey."

Jeremy snorted. "Harvir's a soccer man," he said.

"Same diff," scoffed Kara.

"Hope it's good," said Jeremy. "I'm coming up soon. Not looking forward to reading my pitiful genius to the class."

Alarm shot through Maddy. This wasn't something she'd considered – *she* was going to have to take her turn, stand in front of the class and read her contribution to the novel as Ken watched her every move. How long was it before her turn arrived? Malone usually appeared halfway down a class list. If a student read every two days.... But Maddy couldn't think straight, her mind spinning and tripping over itself. How was she going to write three hundred words, much less get up and read them, knowing Ken—

"Good afternoon, class," said Ms. Mousumi, cutting into her thoughts. "We've got a lot to cover today, so I'd like to get going on the next chapter of our novel. Harvir, could you come up and read your chapter?"

Muffled snickers rose from the area around Harvir's desk as he stood. Ms. Mousumi moved to her desk and sat down, several feet to Maddy's left.

"Well," said Harvir, ambling to the front of the room. Tall and broad-shouldered, he had the kind of smile that looked ready to befriend anyone. "This chapter is called 'The Soul Stones.'" He glanced at Ms. Mousumi. "Were we supposed to give our chapter a title?"

"That's fine," nodded the teacher.

"Okay," said Harvir. More snickers rose around his vacated desk.

"Class!" snapped Ms. Mousumi.

"Well," said Harvir, nobly ignoring the interruption. "This is kind of weird, but it's what I got. So here goes. 'The Soul Stones.' The high priestess stood in her office." He paused again to shoot a glance at Ms. Mousumi. "I don't know if high priestesses have offices, but I didn't know what else to call it."

"We're with you," assured Ms. Mousumi.

"Okay," said Harvir. "Like I said, she's in her office. She

was alone because it was the middle of the night, with only a crescent moon. There was a table in the middle of the room, with an oil lamp burning. On the table, the high priestess spread out a whole bunch of stones. They were small stones, from a creek near the village. There was a stone for each villager, and the high priestess knew exactly which stone matched which villager.

"Because the high priestess was really a witch. She was an evil witch full of black magic and havoc. Everyone was afraid of her. Before she came to the village, things were hunky-dory. But when she came, she brought in the tradition of the soul stones, and everything started to go wrong. She told the people the gods sent her to take care of their souls. She said the best way to do this was if the people gave their souls to her, and then she could keep them safe.

"This is how she took their souls. She made each villager kneel. Then she put a stone to his forehead, and called his soul out of his body and into the stone. Then she put the stones into a basket in her office. Each time a new baby was born, she put a stone on its forehead—" Here, Harvir stopped and looked up. "Well, *very* carefully, of course, because the baby was little...."

Further snickers erupted and Harvir scowled. "Class!" warned Ms. Mousumi, and the snickers quieted.

"Well," Harvir said disapprovingly, "I should know about a thing like that, because my nephew just got born. Anyway, the witch put a new stone on the new baby's forehead, and took its soul too. Soon she had all of the villagers' souls in her basket in her office.

"When it was the crescent moon, the high priestess-witch took all her soul stones out of the basket and spread them out on her table. She put them in circles and geometric designs, like squares and triangles, and eight-pointed stars and stuff. Then she called down blessings or curses from the gods into the stones and their souls, depending on whether she liked a certain person. The blessings and curses always worked. The witch knew what she was doing. You sure wouldn't want to run into her in a dark alley, ever.

"But you're probably wondering about the heroine of our story – Farang, the pain eater. What has this all got to do with her? Well, the high priestess-witch didn't like Farang. Actually, she didn't really like anyone, that's the kind of person she was. Very grumpy. And like Kara said in her chapter, it was Farang's job to feel pain. So the high priestess *always* cursed Farang. She put Farang's stone in the middle of the table and made sure she called the greatest evil down upon *her* soul. Which was pretty tough on Farang, I must say. Because, of course, Farang had the curses the high priestess put on her, *plus* later on she got all the other villagers' pain at the full moon – which meant all *their* curses too. Farang was getting a bum deal out of life, no two ways about it. And she was the only one who knew it.

"Because, you see, the high priestess only called curses into the soul stones deep in the dark dark night, when everyone was asleep. Almost everyone in the tribe slept at night – everyone except Farang. Because no one watched over Farang. She had no mother or father, so she could stay awake all night if she wanted. So she did – she stayed awake at night and spied on the high priestess. So she saw the witch cursing the stones. And then she saw the villagers suddenly getting leprosy, or falling off a cliff, or being attacked by a tiger. The villagers *suspected* – they guessed the high priestess was out to get them. But only Farang *saw* the way it happened. Only she *knew* for sure. And she couldn't tell anyone, because they weren't allowed to talk to her.

"So that was the tribe's biggest problem. Poor Farang knew what it was. She knew *exactly* what their greatest danger was – the high priestess, who the villagers trusted with their souls. They trusted the witch, but not the person who could tell them the truth. How will this problem be solved? Who will save this village from the evil tyrant, the high priestess? Tune in to the next chapter in order to find out all the exciting answers to your questions."

Harvir glanced up with a shy grin, then made a sweeping bow. Whistles erupted from the back row, and the class broke into a round of applause. Sheepishly, Harvir handed his crumpled pages to Ms. Mousumi, and they stood talking for a moment.

"Well?" demanded Jeremy, turning in his seat to shoot Kara an inquiring glance.

"Not bad," Kara said grudgingly. "Definitely better than I thought it'd be."

"Wonder who's next," muttered Jeremy, scanning the room. "There's gotta be a few B and C names."

"Paul Benitez – can you have your chapter ready for Monday?" asked Ms. Mousumi, directing her question at a chubby boy three desks to Maddy's right. Paul shot bolt upright, his panicky expression setting off a wave of laughter. "Class! Class!" Ms. Mousumi called sharply. "I expect respect at all times! Now – Paul, how are you for Monday?"

Paul gave a jerky nod.

"Fine," said Ms. Mousumi. "And after that, it'll be Vince Cardinal on Wednesday, and—"

"Excuse me, Ms. Mousumi?" said Ken Soong, raising his hand. "You skipped Julie – Julie Armstrong, right over here. She should come after Harvir, shouldn't she?"

Two desks over, Julie reached around David Janklow and swatted Ken on the arm.

"Yes, yes," said Ms. Mousumi, consulting her attendance sheet. "Of course. Thank you, Ken. So it'll be Julie Armstrong on Monday, Paul on Wednesday, and Vince Cardinal next Friday. And the following Monday, it's Christine Considine. All right, class. I think Harvir gave us an exciting sequel to Kara's excellent beginning. We'll look forward to Julie's contribution. Now, if you'll turn to…."

Beside Maddy, Kara leaned forward and poked Jeremy in the back. "Slacker," she hissed. "So you get two weeks. Then it's your turn with the firing squad."

"Maybe she'll skip me by mistake," Jeremy muttered back.

"Not a chance," said Kara. "Not with the eye I've got pinned to your back."

Slouched one seat to Kara's left, Maddy wedged her right thumbnail pain-deep into the back of her left hand.

chapter three

They were on her. Feet pounded up from behind, hands grabbed, voices grunted. Terror surged through Maddy, a flock of birds exploding every which way. *No!* she thought, trying to push back against the bodies that pressed in on her. *Please, no!* But a hand clapped itself across her mouth, a hand that shut down sound. She couldn't speak—

Breath tearing her lungs, gasping, Maddy came awake and sat bolt upright in bed. Whimpers skittered from her mouth, followed by a long grinding whine. *Yeah, you like it,* hissed a voice in her head. *Don't play hard to get with us.* White masks leered, their identical features luminescent in the dark. Groping desperately, Maddy clicked on her bedside reading lamp. Light attacked her eyes; half-blinded, she sat blinking, then pulled open a drawer in the small table next to her bed. The pack of cigarettes lay hidden under a notebook. She extracted one and lit up; then, without hesitating, she brought the glowing ember down to her left inner thigh.

The pain was immediate – sharp-edged and gouging her flesh. Eyes smarting, Maddy held herself rigid, her entire being focused on the ember's brilliance, that enemy-friend teaching her flesh. Teaching it to be strong, teaching it to overcome. Teaching it to destroy, to take what had come before and turn it into nothing…gone now. Gradually, as Maddy sat holding agony a hair's breadth from her skin, the voices in her head, the grabbing hands, faded from her mind. Just as it faded from her flesh – flesh that insisted on reliving every sensation she'd felt during the rape, so her arms and legs ached as if freshly bruised, and between her legs….

But fire cleared all of that. Fire was a cleanser. Fire took away memory and pain, and what it left behind was nothing – a pure, blessed numbness that poured itself through Maddy like the water that followed fire and put it out. Emptied of pain, emptied of all sensation, she sat staring at the cigarette she now held midair before her face, watching the ember wisp out. On her left thigh, a heat blister was rising, an angry red weal surrounded by pink, healed-over scars. Seventeen – Maddy didn't have to count to know this blister was the seventeenth on her left thigh, or that she had eight on her right. None of them hurt now the numbness had come, and that was all that mattered – that nothing hurt, that she feel nothing at all.

Maddy butted out the cigarette in an ashtray she kept hidden on her bookshelf. Then she headed to the bathroom for some Polysporin and a bandage to cover the memory of what she could not seem to forget.

• • •

Monday afternoon, English buzzed with the usual chatter. Head down, Maddy scurried across the front of the room and sank into her seat. One row ahead, Jeremy Dugger had turned around and was talking to Kara, who paid him little heed. From the far side of the room, a hyena laugh sounded, high-pitched with a hysterical edge. Maddy didn't have to look up to identify the laugher – Harvir was famous for his manic giggle – but still she did, her gaze flicking across the rear row to the right of the doorway.

And found herself looking straight into the eyes of Ken Soong – hard, direct, and right on her. Not only Ken – beside him, David Janklow also had his gaze pinned on Maddy, his expression less intense, more…. Dropping her own eyes, Maddy focused on watching her right thumbnail drive itself deep into the back of her left hand. The shakes – she couldn't get the shakes. Not here, not now. *Get a grip, get a grip!* she thought. Heartbeat – why did they call it that? It was more like being body-slammed from the inside out. Were they still looking – Ken and that other guy, David Janklow? Why was David looking at her? Did he know about what happened last March? Had Ken told him?

She *had* to know – Maddy had to know if Ken and David were still watching, but she could feel the heat pulsing in her face. She was beet red, she knew it, and if she glanced up now, the nuclear fusion lighting her up would be a dead giveaway. As soon as Ken saw, he'd know. He'd know for sure that she knew…what? A frown creased Maddy's forehead, and her thoughts slowed. Last March, all five of her attackers had been wearing masks. Which meant they'd probably assumed she'd never guess their identities. And even if they hadn't assumed this, there was no way they could know for sure that she'd figured out three of them from their voices – Ken from the get-go, and Pete and Robbie from overhearing them later in the halls.

Why hadn't she thought of this before? It changed everything. Bathed in relief, Maddy sat mulling over this revelation: Ken didn't know that she knew he'd been involved. And if Ken didn't know, none of them did. Which meant, she thought giddily, she was safe. Because if she couldn't identify them, *they* were safe, and as long as they were safe, they'd leave her alone. All Maddy had to do was act as if Ken was no one in particular – just another guy – and she'd be okay. None of the five would bother her again, and she wouldn't bother them.

A finger floated gently through Maddy's thoughts, and touched the back of her left hand. "Why do you do that?" asked Kara, tracing one of several fresh welts.

Convulsively, Maddy jerked her hand away. "Do what?" she mumbled, her eyes on her lap. "I'm not doing anything."

Kara's hand retreated. Her tone, when she replied, was carefully noncommital. "Sure," she said. "Whatever." She went back to her phone.

The classroom chatter was cut by Ms. Mousumi's voice. "Class," she said. "We're about to begin. Julie, please come up and read your chapter."

A low cheer rose from the area around Julie's desk. As

she stood and made her way to the whiteboard, Maddy didn't bother looking up. She knew, without checking, the exact contours of the smirk that would be parading across the other girl's face. That smirk was always there – Julie seemed to consider it a basic fashion accessory. Or, perhaps, a personality accessory. Certainly, Maddy would have been the first to agree that the smirk suited Julie. Smirks didn't belong on every face, but on Julie's, a smirk looked home-grown.

"Okay," said Julie, consulting the tablet in her hand. "*The Pain Eater*, chapter three. Here we go. Poor Farang. Not only did she have no friends, but she was ugly. She was so ugly that even if she hadn't been the pain eater, still no one would've talked to her. So her fate was doubly sad – not only did no one like her, but she couldn't even like herself, because she hated her own face."

Beside Maddy, Kara gave a quiet hiss. "Figures," she muttered.

"But here's the weird thing," continued Julie, her voice taking on a sing-song quality. "When Farang ate the allura leaf poison and felt all that pain, she went away from it. She went away from the pain and the way no one loved her, to a place she made up inside her head. This place was a place of beauty and love, where everyone was kind to her and was her friend. She was beautiful there – so beautiful, suitors came from far and wide to ask for her hand. Farang loved this place, and she called it 'The Beautiful Land.'

"But the thing about The Beautiful Land is that it only came alive when she ate the allura poison and was in horrible pain. She had to feel pain like lightning shooting through her first. She had to be sweating buckets and screaming before she could see The Beautiful Land inside her head. No matter how hard she tried to imagine it at other times, The Beautiful Land just wouldn't come to her then. The Beautiful Land and the pain went together, and that was all there was to it. 'No pain, no gain,' as the saying goes.

"And so Farang started to love pain. Because that was the only time she was happy. It was the only time she was beautiful. Sure, it wasn't real, but what did that matter? And sure, too, she had to feel some of the terrible pain first, before she could go to The Beautiful Land in her head. But then she *was* gone into The Beautiful Land, and when she was there, she couldn't feel the pain anymore. Mind over matter, I guess, but if your life is as down-and-out as Farang's, you might as well.

"So now we know – Farang loved her pain. It worked for her, it got her what she wanted. So, really, we shouldn't feel too sorry for Farang. She was happy, sort of, in a weird way. And she was helping the tribe out – she was feeling their pain for them and taking care of their problems. So she had her place in life, and it was a good thing for everyone.

"So that's the end of my chapter on Farang, the pain eater. Farang, the ugly pain eater, who got high on her own pain. It was like a drug to her, a beautiful poison. That poison was her best friend, really. And we all know besties are hard to come by. So hang on to them when you find them, and count your blessings the way Farang counted hers. She knew she was good for something. She was happy with her fate."

Silence followed the end of Julie's reading – dense, absolute. All across the room, no one spoke; no one seemed even to be breathing. Head down, Maddy stared at her hands. *Wrong* – something was wrong with what she'd just heard, and it was more than the smirk that had been riding Julie's mouth. But what was it? What were the words to put to the confusion she felt shifting around inside?

"Okay, that's everything," said Julie, turning to Ms. Mousumi with a questioning look. "Can I sit down?"

Before the teacher could reply, Kara's hand shot up. "Excuse me," she said.

"Yes, Kara?" said the teacher.

"Well," said Kara, her tone clipped. "That's *not* the way the story was set up. It's just not the way it should go."

Julie's ever-present smirk faltered. "Why not?" she asked.

Kara took a sharp breath. "The first chapter didn't say what Farang looked like, so I guess it's okay she doesn't look as beautiful as you," she snapped. "But I didn't say the pain was *good*. Plus, I said Farang *didn't* believe in her fate – that was the point of my last sentence, remember?"

A flush colored Julie's face. "So things changed," she shrugged. "The plot is getting better. Anyway, you only get to decide what goes on in the first chapter, not the whole thing."

"Yeah, but you have to follow what's gone before!" burst out Kara. "You can't just go ahead and pretend it never happened!"

"I didn't—" Julie started to reply, but Ms. Mousumi cut her off.

"Okay, ladies," said the teacher. "Things are getting personal, but I do think an interesting point has been raised. What does the rest of the class think? Has Julie moved too far away from the plot and characterization as it was established in chapters one and two? Julie, you can sit down now, thanks."

Julie returned to her seat in the midst of a thinking silence. In the back row, two desks over from Maddy, a hand went up.

"Yes, Theresa?" asked Ms. Mousumi.

"I think it's okay about pain causing The Beautiful Land and all that," said a heavyset girl with glasses. "That's interesting, and it can happen in real life. I read about it in *A House in the Sky* – that book by Amanda Lindhout, where she gets tortured in Somalia. She made up things in her head to survive her pain, sort of like Julie made Farang do. But I think Kara's right too – if she said Farang doesn't believe in suffering for the tribe anymore, that's how the rest of us have to write about her."

"Weeeeell," drawled Julie, "I didn't say she *did* believe in suffering for the tribe. I just—"

"You said she was happy with her fate," interrupted Theresa. "Farang can't be happy with her fate if she doesn't believe in it."

Julie's smirk went into another falter, and she slouched down in her seat.

"Any response to that, Julie?" asked Ms. Mousumi.

"Not really, I guess," said Julie. "Except that I thought that when it was *my* turn, I was supposed to take the story where *I* thought it should go. I didn't know I had to worry about keeping *Kara* happy."

Kara hissed something indecipherable under her breath.

"Does anyone else have a comment?" asked Ms. Mousumi. Another hand went up. "Yes, Harvir?"

"I thought Julie's chapter was okay," said Harvir, a diplomatic expression on his face. "I'm not taking it personally that she didn't mention the high priestess or the soul stones. She just added a new twist, like I did."

"It's twisted, all right," muttered Kara.

And it was, thought Maddy. Kara was completely and totally correct – Julie's version of the story *was* twisted. Hunched in her seat, Maddy could feel the wrongness of Julie's chapter almost writhing inside her. But *why* was it wrong? And what were the exact words to describe the wrongness of it?

"Anyone else?" asked Ms. Mousumi, her gaze roaming the class. But she didn't see. She didn't see the thoughts raging inside Maddy, the words so close to forming on the tip of her tongue.

"All right then," said the teacher. "We'll leave it there for today. Paul – you're next, with chapter four on Wednesday."

And the class moved on.

chapter four

Maddy sat on the living-room couch, sketchbook on her knees. She was drawing her father, who was seated at the opposite end of the couch, watching an episode of *Mad Men*. Her mother sat across the room at the family computer, catching up on email. Upstairs in her bedroom, Leanne was working on homework and refusing to speak to Maddy. Maddy, in response, was pretending not to notice.

"Delores, you remember the charity dinner at the Hilton this Saturday?" Mr. Malone asked as some ads came on.

"Mmm hmm. My dress is at the cleaner's," replied Ms. Malone. "Does your good suit need cleaning?"

"Pressing," said Mr. Malone. "But I can get Maddikins to do that, right, m'dear?" Turning, he winked at Maddy. "Five bucks. How's that sound?"

"Ten," said Maddy, slitting her eyes at him. "And I need

your profile. Quit wobbling your mustache."

"That's called a smile, sweetie," said her father. "And this is called a ten-dollar scowl. Since when do fathers have to pay ten bucks to get their pants ironed?"

Maddy sat, lips pursed, thinking. "Five bucks per leg," she offered. "The jacket's extra."

With a shout of laughter, her father lunged, grabbing her in a bear hug. "I'll five bucks you!" he roared. "This is a five-buck tickle!"

His fingers darted across Maddy's back and under her arms, in search of her ribs. Maddy raised both hands to protect herself, and her sketchbook and pencil dropped to the floor. She had always been ticklish, a primary target for her father's teasing. By the time Leanne had reached high school, she'd convinced Ian Malone that his elder daughter was too old for his "shock and awe campaigns," but Maddikins was his baby, the twinkle in his eye. He could resign himself to Leanne's firmly announced adult status; Maddy was another matter entirely.

But Maddy couldn't breathe. Her nose and mouth were clear, and her father wasn't holding her tightly, yet the instant his arms had slid around her, all the air seemed to have been sucked out of the room. With it had gone the light; she couldn't see, everything was going dark, and they were closing in on her – their grunting voices, the panting, the hands that grabbed and shoved. Terror exploded through her; it shouted up her throat. Pushing hard, Maddy kicked out with her feet. "Whoa!" cried a voice and the grabbing hands withdrew, the weight pressing her down pulled back. Breath returned to Maddy in huge, gulping sobs. She couldn't get enough of it – heaved and *heaved* with the effort of breathing free air.

"Maddy?" came a tentative voice, followed by a hand touching her hair. Maddy jerked away, whimpering, and the voice said, "Okay, okay, Maddy. It's okay. You're okay."

It was her mother. Eyes squeezed shut, still sucking in air, Maddy recognized her mother's voice but couldn't open to it. Not yet. "No," she whimpered. "No, no, *no*."

"Okay, Maddy," whispered her mother. "Take your time. Try and calm down, okay, honey?"

Breathing was getting better now, the air not so impossible to reach. Maddy shuddered, shuddered again. Slowly, she opened her eyes. At the far end of the couch sat her father, looking astounded. In front of her knelt her mother, eyes like searchlights, scanning Maddy's every breath. "Honey," she said. "Sweetie, are you okay?"

Maddy blinked, sniffed, then wiped her runny nose on her sleeve. Her face was wet with tears. "Sorry," she mumbled. "I freaked. I didn't mean to."

"No, *I'm* sorry, Maddikins," said her father. "I didn't mean…." His voice trailed off, then he burst out again, "I'm sorry!"

"Can I get you some tea?" asked her mother. "Peppermint with honey – your favorite?"

"I'll get it," her father said quickly. "Let me, Del."

Getting to his feet, he exited the room. For a moment, Delores Malone knelt motionless, then rose and sat beside Maddy on the couch. "May I?" she asked, taking Maddy's right hand. Head down, Maddy sat, feeling her mother gently run a thumb across the back of her hand – a bedtime gesture Delores Malone had used years ago to stroke her youngest daughter to sleep. Gradually, the tension left Maddy's shoulders and eased out of her chest. Pulling her hand free, she yanked a Kleenex out of a nearby box and blew her nose.

Her father came in with a mug of tea. It was the blue mug with the mauve flower – her favorite. She took a sip, followed the warmth down her throat.

"Okay?" asked her father, sitting down on the other side of her mother.

Maddy nodded. "I'm sorry," she said again, keeping her eyes closed. "It wasn't you. I just freaked. I don't know why."

Her parents glanced at one another. "You're sure, Maddy?" probed her mother. "You can't think of some reason? Nothing's happened? Noth—"

Panic surged up Maddy's throat and shattered across her brain. She *couldn't* talk about it. She couldn't think – even *think* about it. "No!" she shouted at her mother, her eyes now wide open and watching her parents' faces tighten with alarm. "Nothing's happened! Nothing's wrong! I don't want to talk about it. Leave me alone. Just leave me goddamn alone."

Her parents sat stiffly, staring straight ahead. Tears slid, glistening, down her mother's cheeks. "Maddy," she whispered.

But Maddy didn't know how to respond.

• • •

Paul Benitez was a case of nerves. As he stood at the front of the class, he looked ready to leapfrog out of his skin. His glasses slid down his nose; pushing them back up, he left a large, sweaty fingerprint at the center of one lens. About to start, he cleared his throat, then went into an extended coughing fit. "Sorry," he choked, turning toward the whiteboard to hide his flushed face.

Snickers rose from the desks around the classroom door. *Julie, of course*, thought Maddy, with a flash of anger. *And probably Harvir and...the rest of them.* Why couldn't they lay off for once? Take one day off for mercy?

"Take your time, Paul," Ms. Mousumi said quietly.

Paul flashed her a glance of pure misery. Squinting at the single squashed page in his hand, he croaked, "Okay. Here goes. Pain. What is it like to eat pain? What does it taste like? Does it taste different on different days, or is it always the same? We know Farang's pain was from the allura leaf, so maybe hers always tasted the same. But is that true for everyone?

"Because we all eat pain. Oh, yes – every one of us eats pain. Not every day, maybe, but we all do sometimes. How do we eat pain? Do we even know we're eating it when we do? Pain is invisible, but you can still taste it. You can feel it in your stomach. I think it tastes somewhere between lightning and acid. It lights up your whole brain like sticking your finger in a socket. Then it's like tasting a scream.

"No one wants to taste a scream. It's okay to watch someone else screaming in a movie, but you don't want it to be you. So that's why you look for someone else to give your pain to.

You make someone else eat your pain, like Farang's tribe did to her. You kick the dog or pick on your little brother, and then you feel better. Why is that? How can hurting someone else take away your own hurt?

"I wonder if Farang's tribe even thinks about this. Do any of them feel guilty for what they do to her? Do any of them want to be friends with her? But then they would have to eat their own pain again. They would have to stop hurting her, and feel their own hurt.

"Maybe it's because of the soul stones. Maybe the tribe can't stop hurting Farang because they don't have their souls anymore. Someone has to rescue their souls for them, please. But I know what I'm going to do. I'm going to stop kicking my dog from now on."

Paul stood a moment, staring at the page in his hand, then bolted for his desk. As he passed behind her, Maddy ducked, then turned to watch him collapse into his seat three desks over. Across the classroom, silence sat heavily. Students sat staring at their desks, or shooting sideways glances at Paul.

"Well," said Ms. Mousumi, getting to her feet. "Thank you, Paul. That was very…thoughtful. Any comments?"

Kara's hand shot up. "I liked it!" she said, her voice so intense it punched the air. "I think it was really great."

Another hand went up. "I liked it too," said a girl named Lilian Pickersgill. "But it wasn't really a *story*, was it? I mean, how did it fit into the novel?"

"That doesn't matter," said Kara. "It had to do with pain-eating, didn't it?"

Ms. Mousumi nodded. "In a collective novel, format is going to change, depending on the contributor. I think it fits in with the overall theme. Come talk to me at the end of the class, Paul – I need to get a copy of your chapter."

Paul nodded, his chubby face a brilliant red. He looked about to cry, and at the same time fiercely proud – as if he'd accomplished some great, good thing. Watching him, Maddy felt a rush of gladness so pure it felt like light along the edge of a glass. Paul's awkward, stumbling chapter was, she realized, the most important thing she'd ever heard. In her entire life, she didn't expect to hear anything truer. *Or braver*, she thought, glancing again at his flushed face.

Fingers touched the back of her left hand. "Hey," said Kara. "You're not doing it today."

Surprise took Maddy as she realized her left hand was clear of fingernail welts. "It's just a habit," she muttered, not looking at Kara. "No big deal."

Kara's hand withdrew. Very quietly, as Ms. Mousumi began speaking, Kara said, "Turning your hand into hamburger meat – why would you want to do that to yourself?"

• • •

Maddy sat in a washroom cubicle, pondering Kara's words: *Turning your hand into hamburger meat.* It was forty-five minutes after the comment had been made, and English had just ended – English, last class of the day…a class Maddy had spent endlessly rerunning her classmate's question inside her head: *Why would you want to do that to yourself?*

The back of her left hand was once again covered with red welts. Maddy tilted her hand and studied the indentations. It wasn't a great habit, she knew that. At the same time, it didn't do permanent damage. At least it didn't leave scars like…. Shaking her head, she pushed away the thought. The question was, how obvious was her thumbnail-attack habit? Had anyone besides Kara noticed? Kara was unusually smart, so hopefully not. And the back of Maddy's hand usually recovered by the time she got home, so she was pretty sure none of her family had clued in. She was careful never to do it there….

The washroom door opened and someone came in – two girls, from the sounds of it. Books and laptops thumped onto the counter, and one of them swore. "I thought that class would never end," drawled a familiar voice. "Could you believe Benitez's chapter? I thought he was going to take a crap up there."

It was Julie, a smirk crawling all over her words. In her head, Maddy could see Julie leaning into the mirror and examining her pretty reflection.

"Kicking his dog!" sneered a second voice. "He couldn't kick the broad side of a barn."

"Maybe a veeeery broad barn," Julie replied, and the two girls laughed. Brain on overdrive, Maddy struggled to identify the second girl, then suddenly knew – Dana Ferwerda, a jock who sat next to Julie in English. "This whole collective novel thing is getting on my nerves," continued Julie. "Everyone's taking it so seriously. And that Kara acts like it's her personal property – she gets to run the whole thing just because she came up with the first chapter. Every time someone reads, she's got to pronounce judgment."

"Yeah, she's got some attitude," Dana agreed.

"Couple years from now, she'll be running for president of Student Council," moaned Julie. "Then she'll take over the entire school. Fate worse than preggers."

"Maybe," said Dana.

"What d'you mean maybe?" demanded Julie. "You want a President Ado*spazi*o?"

Dana snickered. "No," she said. "I mean maybe she'll go through a change of attitude, and we'll be spared."

"Yeah," snorted Julie. "Her attitude is rock solid as the Canadian Shield."

"So we change it," Dana said lightly.

Silence descended upon the washroom, so dense Maddy could practically hear Julie thinking her way through it. "And how do you suggest we do that?" Julie asked finally.

"There's ways," said Dana. "Many ways. But we can start with the damn *Pain Eater*."

"Like how?" asked Julie.

"Make it go *our* way," said Dana. "Talk to the kids coming up, *in-flu-ence* them."

Julie broke into a startled laugh. "Who's next?" she asked. "Vince Cardinal, right? Then Christine."

"Yeah," said Dana. "And there's Dugger. Any other Ds?"

Julie thought a moment. "There's that du Pont kid. Does that make him a D or a P?"

Confusion kept them quiet, pondering. "I dunno,"

admitted Dana. "But I don't think there are any Es, and then come the Fs. And the Fs fuckin' rule!"

"Hey!" crowed Julie, and a loud clap followed. *Probably a high-five*, thought Maddy. "You know why I like your mind?" giggled Julie. "It's evil. As evil as mine."

"Birds of a feather," drawled Dana.

It was at this point that Maddy's phone went off. Heart in a supersonic thud, she grabbed for her jeans pocket, which lay somewhere in the rumple surrounding her ankles. Five full seconds of "O Canada" blared before she had the phone in her hands and managed to shut off the ringtone. Why, oh why, had she chosen the national anthem? It had seemed funny at the time, but blasting out of a high school washroom cubicle….

Silence greeted the anthem's sudden death. Under the cubicle door, Maddy watched a pair of runners approach and come to a halt. "Who's in there?" demanded Julie.

Maddy sat riding out the thud of her heart and considering her options. Nothing remotely positive presented itself, so she kept her mouth shut. Damn that phone! If she didn't need it, she'd flush—

"I *said*, who's in there?" repeated Julie.

Maddy continued to sit motionless, vibrating with each heartbeat. Beyond the cubicle, she heard a whisper; then Julie's face appeared at an angle in the space under the door. At the same moment, a rustling sounded to Maddy's left, and she glanced up to see Dana peering over the top of the adjoining cubicle wall.

"Maddy!" said Julie, staring up at her. "It's Maddy, the Mad Eavesdropper."

"I wasn't eavesdropping," said Maddy. "I was tinkling."

"Mighty quiet tinkle," observed Dana, her eyes narrowing.

"I'm a quiet tinkler," said Maddy.

"Quiet as a rock," said Dana. "You could've said something – coughed or made a noise to let us know you were there."

"I thought it'd be rude to fart," said Maddy. The second this left her mouth, she knew it was numbskull. A joke was *not* the way to go here. Abject humility had more survival possibilities.

"You're dead meat, Maddy," said Julie.

Hunching her shoulders, Maddy erected a shell of silence and crawled inside.

"Get out here, or we're coming in," Julie added.

"Paper towels," said Dana, when Maddy gave no sign of moving. "We'll soak them and plaster her with them."

Both faces disappeared, and Maddy heard the sound of running water. "Okay, Maddy," said Julie. "We're coming to get you."

But just as Maddy heard someone step up onto the next toilet seat, the outer washroom door opened and several loudly chattering girls came in. "What's going on here?" demanded a voice.

"None of your business," came Julie's cool reply. "*If* you know what's good for you."

Two pairs of feet exited the washroom, and the outer door swung shut after them. "That's Armstrong's kid sister," observed someone. "I hear she's a megalomaniac."

"Armstrong genes," commented someone else. "Hey – are you okay in there?" A hand knocked on Maddy's cubicle door.

"Yeah," Maddy said weakly. "Good timing, though. Thanks." Pulling up her jeans, she exited her cubicle to find three seniors leaning against the counter opposite.

"Maddy!" exclaimed one of them. "What was that all about?"

It was Tina Snooks, a friend of Leanne's – better known as just *Snooks*. "Nothing much," said Maddy. "Still, I'm glad you walked in when you did."

"You sure?" asked Snooks, waggling her eyebrows. "I can have a little chat with those two, if you'd like. I have connections."

High on relief, Maddy giggled. "No, it was just a fluke kind of thing. They're not after me or anything."

"Well, let me know if you need any *assistance*," said Snooks, heading for a cubicle. "I'll call out my network."

Thanking her lucky stars, Maddy headed out into the hall.

chapter five

There it was, suddenly, on her phone screen – a simple Greek comedy mask, white and leering. She'd been sitting on her bed, checking her Twitter, and the image of the mask had leapt out at her. Stunned, all she could do was stare at it. This mask appeared to be an exact replica of the ones that were handed out at *Our Town,* as if someone had taken a photograph of one of those and tweeted it to her. If so, there could be only one reason: they were after her again, or at least one of them was. Which meant that it wasn't over. They hadn't forgotten her. She hadn't managed to convince them she'd never talk, their secret was safe with her.

No text accompanied the image, except the hashtag #themaskedavengers. The username was @theneverknowns. How had @theneverknowns gotten hold of her username? @Yummibreakfast didn't identify her in any way; had Leanne given it to someone? Or Jennifer, or one of her other friends?

Perhaps. Neither her sister nor her friends would've known, after all, why the guy was asking. But why hadn't they mentioned it? A whimper crept up Maddy's throat; panic resonated through her in waves. Nowhere was safe, she thought. Not here, not anywhere. If @theneverknowns had her username, they could get through to her any time.

Dropping her phone onto the bed, Maddy took off for the tree house, where there was no wifi; no one could reach her, she truly was safe. The backyard and the ladder steps passed in a blur; she clicked on a flashlight she kept with her art supplies and then she was sitting, her head pressed to her knees and hugging her legs. Tighter, *tighter* she hugged, trying to compress her fear, her heartbeat, *herself*, into nothing. But it wasn't working. In spite of her fiercest efforts, memory was starting to unfold and take shape – memory that was stronger than her, stronger and bigger and out to devour.

Another whine ground out of her, and Maddy lifted her head to glare at the chalk mural opposite. *Goddamn sunflowers!* she thought. *Parading their sunlit happy heads!* And that picture of her family, sitting on a dock with a picnic lunch – it was bullshit! La la land! Rising to her knees, Maddy launched herself across the tree house and attacked the pastel family scene, swiping at it repeatedly with her arm. Then she moved on to the sunflowers. The images surrendered easily, smudging to blurs of sky blue, emerald, and saffron. But the memory in her head wouldn't follow suit – no matter how many chalk fantasies she destroyed, the shadows in her mind continued to come after her, feet pounding, hands reaching.

It wasn't enough. Nothing was enough – nothing she could tell herself, no advice, no calm-down talk, no reasonable common sense. Only one thing worked; only one solution took it all away. Crawling over to her art supplies, Maddy pulled out a concealed pack of cigarettes. Then she lit up, inhaled, and raised the hem of her shorts. The terror in her mind was still with her – even as she brought the brilliant ember to her inner thigh, she felt herself being pushed down to frozen ground and hands shoving apart her legs. But then pain took over – pain that gouged, twisted, dug into her flesh. Pain that was a master, a fiery fury that went after everything – chasing it down, kicking it into nothingness, defeating and destroying it. So that, finally, there was nothing left – nothing but numbness spreading out from the fresh blister taking shape on her skin. Nothing but the sweat that beaded her forehead, and the long shuddering breaths that eased slowly out. Exhaustion lapped through Maddy, like waves on a shoreline. Over, it was over now, gone away, and she was at peace. *Peace.* The mural opposite was in pieces, but pieces for peace, she thought wearily – it was a good deal, wasn't it? Just so long as she could get a grip, keep everything together and functioning okay. Wasn't that what was expected, what she was supposed to do?

Another breath shuddered through her. Blinking back tears, Maddy smoked silently.

• • •

Vince Cardinal didn't seem all that interested in what he was reading. Short, with black, shoulder-length hair and glasses, he rattled off the text on his tablet as if he were reading from a phone book. As he progressed, Maddy shot several glances at Julie and Dana, but their bored expressions didn't show much interest either. If they were still planning on influencing the plot's development, they didn't appear to have started with Vince.

Once, Maddy caught Julie watching *her*, but only once. Dana appeared to have forgotten the washroom incident entirely. Neither girl had approached Maddy since it had taken place, two days previous. Though Julie sat only two desks over from Ken, Maddy made sure her glances at the girl didn't take in any part of him. If Ken was watching her – if he was, indeed, the one who'd tweeted the photograph of the mask he seemed to have saved since the rape last March – she didn't want to know.

Maddy's phone was in the drawer of her bedside table. She hadn't looked at it since she'd shoved it in there, after returning from the tree house last night.

"The high priestess sang creepy little songs as she played with the soul stones," Vince read off rapid-fire. "None of them were songs Farang knew, because the high priestess had learned them in a secret language taught only to priestesses. She learned it at a temple school in the capital city of Faraway. That was where all priestesses got their BAs in temple stuff. A high priestess had a PhD.

"So when Farang hid and watched the high priestess hex the soul stones, she couldn't understand the words to the songs. But she did learn which stones went with which villagers. One night, she saw the high priestess pick out a stone that belonged to a great warrior. The high priestess put it at the center of a circle of stones. Then she poured something over the warrior's stone. The liquid smelled awful, like something rotten. Like *death*. It was so awful, Farang almost choked. But she didn't, which was good, because then the high priestess would've killed her.

"The next day Farang hung around the warrior, watching to see what happened. She saw him pick up his bow and arrow and go into the forest. She followed him. Because he was a great warrior, he moved quickly and she couldn't keep up. And so she got further and further behind. BUT!" For the first time, Vince showed interest in what he was reading. Leaning forward, he enunciated carefully. "THEN FARANG SAW THE HIGH PRIESTESS STEP INTO A CLEARING. THE HIGH PRIESTESS GOT ONTO HER HANDS AND KNEES AND CHANGED INTO A TIGER. THEN THE TIGER TOOK OFF AFTER THE WARRIOR.

"Farang didn't know what to do," Vince continued, his voice returning to normal. "She was too far behind the warrior to warn him. And if the high priestess saw *her*, she might kill her instead of the warrior. So Farang went back to the village. The next day, when the warrior's dead body was brought into the village, she saw the claw marks all over him. The high priestess had gotten him all right. The great warrior was the only villager who would argue with her. So she killed him.

"Farang was the only one who knew this. Everyone else thought it was a real tiger. And Farang couldn't tell them. If she tried, they wouldn't listen to her. She had to figure out some way of telling the villagers that didn't look like it was coming from her.

"That's what I think, anyway." Lowering his tablet, Vince glanced at Ms. Mousumi and shrugged.

"Thank you, Vince," she said. "Can you send me a copy? Any comments, class?"

As Vince headed to his seat, the class sat, slumped in thought. A hand went up.

"Is shapeshifting something the high priestess learned at the temple?" asked Julie. "Or can anyone in the tribe do it?"

Ms. Mousumi glanced inquiringly at Vince, who made an exasperated face. "Not *anyone*," he replied. "Or why was Farang so shocked?"

"You didn't say she was shocked," Julie pointed out.

Vince frowned. "Well, she was," he said huffily. "Wouldn't you be, if you saw that happen?"

"I'm just saying," said Julie, "if *anyone* could do—"

"Well, they can't," Vince cut her off. "It's just the high priestess with her PhD. That's what taught her how to do that."

"So, are you saying *all* the high priestesses through the whole land could do that?" asked Dana. "They were all evil like this high priestess?"

Kara's hand shot up, and Ms. Mousumi gave her the nod. "That's not in Harvir's chapter," said Kara. "The high priestess before this one wasn't evil. Maybe they all know shapeshifting, but it can be used for good as well as evil. Not *all* the high priestesses are evil."

Harvir's hand went up. "That's true," he said. "I agree with Kara on this one. Shapeshifting could be bad or good – it depends on what you want to do with it."

Julie and Dana grimaced at each other, but didn't comment.

"Well, Christine," said Ms. Mousumi, "I guess it's up to you. You'll be presenting your chapter on Monday."

From her seat next to Dana, Christine nodded. Maddy's gaze flicked from Christine, to Dana, to Julie's satisfied grin, then to Kara, who was slouched beside her, scowling. For a long moment, she considered writing Kara a note and revealing Julie and Dana's plan to her. Maddy wasn't Farang, after all – Kara *would* listen to her, she would be believed.

But once told, Kara would kick up a fuss, no doubt about it – a fuss that would go all the way to Ms. Mousumi. Was this situation worth that kind of fuss? So what if Julie and Dana went around trying to influence the way the story went? It was just a story, after all. Moreover, it was up to each student to decide if they wanted to be influenced. Maddy had more important things to worry about; she had bigger, darker, heavier things on her mind. So she decided not to tell Kara, not to get involved any further, to let things slide.

Lowering her gaze, she concentrated on turning her left hand into hamburger meat.

• • •

Midway along one of the city's riverside bike trails, Maddy braked to a halt. It was windy – the weather report had said thirty mile-per-hour gusts, but these felt more like fifty. Pulling up her jacket hood, she stood a moment, surveying the scene. She was on the higher riverbank, at the top of a bluff, and the city stretched out before her, its streets September-gold, rippling under the ever-present prairie wind. Up here, near the sky, thought Maddy, breath went in deeper, scented with that dry, sweet smell that came only in autumn. But it wouldn't last long. One more week of heavy winds and that golden glory would flee the landscape, leaving a series of browns.

Still, today life was gorgeous-golden, and with her phone lying in her bedside table drawer, she was unreachable. Hood tied tight, Maddy started off along the trail. This time of year, it was crowded with university students, cycling and jogging; she had to keep a constant eye out. Before leaving, she'd thought about asking Leanne to come with her on this Saturday-afternoon ride, but her sister had headed out for a swim with friends, pointedly not inviting Maddy. Even if Leanne had invited her, Maddy would have had to refuse – public pools didn't admit swimmers with open sores on their inner thighs, and, anyway, how would she have explained? Maddy hadn't been swimming once this past summer, not since she'd started playing with fire. Playing and praying – to be cleansed, to be cured.

Not that she wanted to think about that now. Not up here, where everything stretched before her, sun-dappled and wind-sung. Ignoring the throb where her jeans rubbed against her bandaged blisters, Maddy put on a burst of speed, then slowed as the trail dipped and went into a blind curve. Trees crowded in here, the trail having veered away from the river, and the wind had calmed. A bench waited at the curve's apex; stopping her bike, Maddy sat down and got out the Mars bar she had brought along for just such a moment.

A group of cyclists came around the bend to her left, their heads down, their legs pumping. Obviously in a race, the three guys paid her no heed, their voices hoarse as they called friendly insults back and forth. Just as they passed, Maddy recognized the guy in the lead – David Janklow – and then the one right behind him, his head coming up momentarily as he gave a long wolf howl, "Ai-eeeee!" Then the three were past her and shrinking into the distance, their butts dancing over their bike seats as they strove to outpace each other.

Alone on the bench, Maddy stared after them. The way the second cyclist had raised his head, and that long wolf cry – it was familiar, so familiar she'd seen and heard it a hundred times. The first had been last March, as she'd lain trapped against the cold ground; the rest had come via memory. That March night, the third masked rapist had lifted his head exactly the way the second cyclist had just now, and then he'd let out an eerie, ululating howl. He was one of the two Maddy hadn't been able to identify yet; even after seeing his face today, she couldn't put a name to him. But she *had* observed him walking school halls, often in the company of Pete Gwirtzman – so he was probably also in grade eleven. And even though today's glimpse had been brief, she had noted his obvious resemblance to David. Was he an older brother? A cousin?

But of more immediate importance – were David and the

others planning to follow this bike trail across one of the bridges to the other side of the river, or to reverse tracks and come back this way? She had to get out of here, but quick! Shoving her half-eaten chocolate bar into her pocket, Maddy mounted her bike and took off along the trail in the opposite direction to the three cyclists. Within minutes, she was drenched in sweat, her breath rasping and her leg muscles burning. But she kept going, kept her legs pumping mindlessly as she shoved herself away from the afternoon's encounter – away from the memory of it, away from the possibility of it having gone differently, maybe even….

No! She wasn't going to think about that now! Ahead, the bike trail merged with a city street, and five blocks farther was her neighborhood and the sight of her house at the end of a boulevard. Pulling into the driveway, Maddy ditched her bike by the garage without bothering to lock it. Then she ran for the backyard and the tree house, the pack of cigarettes she had hidden behind a sketchbook, and the lighter that would bring the blessed fire and the longed-for, numbed nothingness of mind.

chapter six

Christine Considine smiled brightly at the class. Slender, with long, dark hair, she was pretty enough to be admitted into the fringes of the in-crowd, but not pretty enough to take their tolerance for granted. Now, before starting to read her chapter, she arched an eyebrow at Julie; Julie replied with an answering smirk.

"*The Pain Eater*, instalment for Monday, September 16," Christine recited in a clear, slightly mocking tone. "It was the full moon. As always, the tribe was coming together to dance and sing. Everyone was there – the high priestess and other priestesses, the chief, and all the villagers. Farang was hiding in the bushes, because she didn't get to join in the fun part. But the question is – how much fun was it for everyone else?

"Because remember – the tribe was about to give Farang their pain. That means they had a lot of it. So where did this pain come from? Well, the chief had a son who had some kind of a disease. No one knew what it was, but it made him weak and pale. Lots of times, he couldn't go out hunting. Sometimes he couldn't even get out of bed. He was the chief's only child, so this was a big deal.

"Then there was a woman who was mauled by a tiger – a real one, not the high priestess. Her wounds never healed properly, and they hurt a lot. And there was a little girl who fell out of a tree and got a bad concussion, and a lot of other problems like that. Plus, there were people who were sad because someone they loved died – I mean really, *really* sad. Some people got so sad, they could hardly go on living. So there was a lot of suffering in this tribe, just from their daily lives, not to mention the problems the high priestess dished out.

"And the thing was – Farang made it better. When the people gave her their pain, she took it away and their lives got better. The chief's son got better again, and he could go out hunting with the other men. In fact, he was about to get married and become the new chief because his dad was retiring. So he was important, and the tribe needed him to be well. And the woman who was mauled by the tiger? She was the tribe's best weaver. If she couldn't weave, someone had no clothes. And the little girl with the concussion just made everyone happy. They all loved her to bits. When her concussion acted up and the little girl cried, everyone got upset. She was important to everyone, part of their hearts.

"Everyone was like this, really. The tribe had hundreds of people, and everyone had a secret pain. Lots of them never talked about it – they just gave their pain to Farang, so she was the only one who ever knew about it. Farang knew a lot of secrets, because when someone gave her their pain, she could tell why it was there. Farang knew everyone's secrets – she knew what everyone was hiding from everyone else.

"Think about it – what a person like that means. What if someone in this class knew your deepest secret, a secret you've never told anyone else? Would you want her around? Wouldn't you be worried about her telling someone? And what if this same person knew the deepest secret *of every single person in this class?* That deepest secret you've sworn never to tell anyone. Would you want her sitting next to you like a friend? Would you want her talking away to other people like one of the crowd?

"No – you'd want to make sure she kept her mouth shut. Because if she opened it, who knows what might come out? Be honest – it wasn't just the high priestess who had everyone over a barrel, it was also Farang. All she had to do was open her mouth and start talking, and a lot of people's lives would be wrecked. That would be bad for the tribe. Some secrets are best never told, and the tribe had to make sure Farang never told them. Because that was what was best for the tribe. The tribe was hundreds of people, Farang was only one. Yes, it was hard on her. Yes, she suffered. But she helped a lot of people in the process. So it was all for the good in the end."

Christine gave a satisfied nod to herself, then shot Ms. Mousumi a sideways glance. "That's it," she said. "Here, you can have this copy." Walking over to the teacher's desk, she handed Ms. Mousumi two pages.

"Thank you," said Ms. Mousumi. "You can sit down. Any comments?"

The class sat silent, dense with thought. Beside Maddy, Kara wore a thinking grimace. *Secrets*, Maddy thought, staring down at the thumbnail welts in her hand. *What if someone knew your deepest secret? Would you want her around?* Swiftly, before she could tell herself not to, she glanced at the desks near the door. Alarm leapt through her, inner fire. As expected, Ken was watching her, his eyes fixed in a steady, unblinking stare. Next to him, David Janklow was also watching her, his expression uncertain, his mouth sucked in.

And it hit her then like a searing blast of wind – David was the last unidentified rapist, the fifth Masked Avenger. *No*, Maddy thought, her gaze plummeting. *David didn't rape me. He was the one standing lookout. He never touched me.*

Her heart was body-slamming her from the inside out; she felt exhausted by this new knowledge, as if she could barely remain upright. For two weeks now, she'd been sitting across the room from *two* guys who'd been involved, not just one. And there was also that time David had clipped her shoulder while passing her in the hall. It was creepy, thinking one of her attackers had been so close all this time and she hadn't known it. How was she supposed to protect herself against something like that happening again when reality played tricks on her like this? Nowhere was safe, Maddy thought frantically. Horrible things could happen anywhere, burst out of the ordinary everyday—

Kara's hand went up. "It's interesting," she said, her tone grudging. "I mean what Christine said about Farang knowing secrets, so everyone hates her for it. I can see that happening, sure. But the way Christine wrote it, the story is, like, blaming Farang for that when it says she has everyone over a barrel. As if it's *her* fault. When it isn't."

Christine arched another eyebrow. "In *your* opinion," she said coolly.

"In my opinion *what?*" asked Kara, her tone now definitely on the warpath. "That it's *not* Farang's fault? Are you saying it *is?*"

Uncertainty blew across Christine's face, and she shrugged. Five seconds of silence ticked by as Kara hissed quietly, and then another hand went up. "How does Farang get to know their secrets when they give her their pain?" asked a guy in the front row. "I need to know – I'm doing the next chapter."

"Yes," said Ms. Mousumi. "Brent...Doody, right?"

Brent nodded, then looked expectantly at Christine. She grimaced. "ESP," she said. "Y'know – mental telepathy. *The X-Files.* Stephen King."

"Doo doo doo doo, doo doo doo doo," Harvir sang in a soft, spectral voice. "Make it up, doodoo-Doody. It's a *story.*"

Ms. Mousumi sent him a remonstrative glare as Brent shrugged. "Just wanted to see if there was an actual reason," Brent said.

"Okay," said Ms. Mousumi. "So it's ESP, and Brent is our Wednesday author. Friday, it'll be Jeremy Dugger."

In front of Maddy, Jeremy stiffened, radiating alarm.

"Doo doo doo doo," Kara sang quietly. "That's what you'll be writing, Dugger."

Behind his back, Jeremy gave her the finger. With a quick breath, Maddy glanced again at the back row close to the classroom entrance. Ken and David were both still watching her. Keeper of secrets, keeper of deep, dark truths – Maddy *was* like Farang, she realized that now. She knew Ken's and David's ugliest moment, a moment that might even feel like pain to them. Unlike Farang's situation, however, this one went both ways. For Ken and David also knew Maddy's ugliest moment. And without question, all three of them wanted to keep that moment as secret as secret got – never spoken about, forbidden to even think about, the unhappy face forever hidden behind the cheerful, smiling one.

• • •

"Maddy," said a voice in her bedroom doorway. Maddy looked up from the verbs she was conjugating for French class to see her father, with her mother standing just behind him. Her heart began a warning thud. "Can we come in?" asked her father.

Maddy nodded, and her parents entered. Her mother sat on the edge of the bed. Her father drew up a chair, sat down, and clasped both hands around one knee. He looked nervous – sad, grim, and as if he was about to jump out of himself. Maddy's heartbeat accelerated.

"Honey," said her mother, reaching for her hand. Maddy pulled back, and Delores Malone bit her lip. "Okay," she faltered. "Maddy, sweetheart – we're worried. You haven't been yourself for…well, months now, and we don't know what to do. You won't tell us what's wrong—"

"Nothing's wrong," Maddy said quickly.

"Yes, something is," said her father, his voice hoarse but determined. "It started last year, sometime in the spring. We thought at first it was a phase, something you had to work out on your own. Things seemed to improve in the summer, but it's much worse now. We can't afford to sit back and let this go on, Maddikins. Something's wrong, and it's *very* wrong."

"No, it's not!" cried Maddy, her eyes fixed on her schoolwork. No way was she looking at her parents – they loved her so much, they'd freak if they found out. "I'm just tired," she mumbled. "I need a break. Maybe if you stopped bothering—"

"We're not going to stop bothering you," interrupted her father. "That's what parents are for. They bother you because they love you. Period."

"Well, I don't want you to bother me!" Maddy said helplessly. "Nothing was wrong before you came in. Now it's horrible. Maybe *you're* the problem."

Her father snorted. "Ian," her mother said. For a moment, all three sat tensed on the edge of what was coming next. "Maddy," said her mother, reaching again for her hand. "We've booked an appointment for you with a Dr. Matusow. She's supposed to be very good – we asked around first. She's worked with a lot of young people. We even met with her ourselves, and we like her."

Confused, Maddy stared at her mother. "What're you talking about?" she demanded, her voice rising. "You want me to see a doctor? But I'm not sick. And we already have a doctor – Dr. Ovason."

"A psychiatrist," said Ms. Malone, looking her straight in the eye. "Dr. Matusow is a psychiatrist who specializes in working with teenagers."

"You want me to see a *psychiatrist?*" Maddy cried. "What – you think I'm crazy?"

"Not crazy," said her father. "No one said anything about crazy."

"Then what?" asked Maddy, her breath harsh in her throat.

Both her parents hesitated, their eyes vague, looking inward. "We don't know what," her mother said finally. "Because you won't tell us. We're hoping you'll tell Dr. Matusow."

Maddy stared at her parents in disbelief. A psychiatrist? Her parents wanted her to see a crazy doctor? No matter what her father said, psychiatrists were for crazies – nutcases who heard voices, then attacked other people on the Greyhound or killed their own kids. Maddy didn't hear voices; she wasn't anywhere near attacking or killing anyone. In fact, she was the one who'd *been* attacked. So why was *she* the one being told to go see a shrink?

"Psychiatrists are doctors for the mind," her mother said soothingly. "Just like your body gets sick sometimes, so can your mind. That's when you need a psychiatrist, Maddy – someone who knows how the mind works. Dr. Matusow will be able to help you. She'll know how to—"

How to get it all out of you, thought Maddy, terror rearing through her. *How to make you talk, how to drag you through every goddamn, fucking second of it all over again.*

"No!" she shouted, rolling onto her side so she faced the wall. "I won't go! I won't!"

Silence followed her words, and then her father cleared his throat. "Maddy, just once," he pleaded. "Just try Dr. Matusow once. See if you like her before you decide."

"No!" Maddy repeated, burying her face in her pillow. "I'm not crazy!"

She could feel it – the way her parents sagged into themselves, defeated. Remorse tore her end to end, but she fought it, refused to turn around and face them.

"Well," her father said slowly, "we won't force you."

Quietly, they stood and left the room.

• • •

As Brent Doody walked to the front of the room, a muffled chant of "Doo doo doo doo" started up from several desks. Seated at her own desk to Maddy's left, Ms. Mousumi raised an eyebrow but didn't comment. Coming to a halt before the class, Brent arranged the pages in his hand and studied the first few lines. Part of the theater crowd, he'd had a minor role in last year's *Bye Bye Birdie*, and had a tendency toward melodrama.

At the back of the room, Julie wore a satisfied expression. Maddy watched her glance at Dana and smirk.

Brent rocked once on his heels. His expression grew suddenly intense. "ZOMBIES!" he cried, leaning forward. "THEY WERE COMING FROM EVERYWHERE! From the huts the people lived in. Out of the forest. From the fields where they worked. Nobody knew why, but every day more and more

71

people in the tribe were turning into zombies. It happened at night. The people went to bed normal, and while they slept, some of them *mutated*.

"Of course, *we* know what was happening. *We* know it was the high priestess causing the problem. Because when you don't have your soul, it's very easy to go over the edge and become a zombie. It can happen in the twinkle of an eye. But the people in the tribe didn't know this. To them, it was a great mystery. Why was this happening, and how? They thought the gods were angry with them. They thought they'd done something wrong.

"When a person turned into a zombie, they stopped doing what they were supposed to. They went psycho! Crazy! Out of their minds! Their eyes glowed orange. All they could think about was eating raw meat. They went after anything, and gobbled it up raw and bloody. Like the tribe's dogs and cats. Or birds. And if they couldn't find those, they'd go after the kids in the tribe. Several babies were missing.

"The tribe was terrified. Every morning, they'd wake up and someone else had gone crazy and was eating babies. Then the whole tribe had to catch the new zombie and kill him. Because if they didn't, he'd eat a baby. This was a major problem. It was getting everyone down.

"Why was the high priestess doing this to the tribe? Because she liked it. The more scared the people got, the more they begged her for help. So she got to be more and more important. Whenever people started to forget about her and maybe not come to the temple so much to pray, she'd turn another few people into zombies. Then everyone would beg her for help, which was exactly what she wanted.

"The high priestess used a very particular stone to zombify people. It was a stone that held the soul of a dead person. This person was a very powerful wizard when he was alive, and the high priestess had beaten him in a duel of magic powers *to the death*. Then she'd put his soul into a stone and brought it with her when she came to this village. Now she was siccing the wizard's soul on the villagers – it was actually his dead soul that was zombifying them.

"Farang spied on the high priestess, and she found out what was going on. One night, she snuck into the office and stole the wizard's soul stone. She took it out into the forest and smashed it into pieces with a bigger rock, and the wizard's soul escaped. Farang could see it lift out of the smashed pieces of rock like a green light. It was eerie.

"'I give you one wish,' it said to her. 'For saving my soul. Because I can read minds, I already know what you most desire. You want to be rich and famous. More powerful than the high priestess. You want to get out of this dinky tribe in this backwoods forest, and go somewhere ritzy and modern where they have toilets and the Internet and democracy. Where you can blow your nose in a Kleenex, for Pete's sake! Well, your wish will be granted. Not right away, but it will come. Be patient. Now, I must go. Before the high priestess wakes up and finds out I'm gone.'

"Before Farang's eyes, he lifted into the air and flew away, leaving her alone. She was angry and shook her fist at him. The wizard was right – he *had* read her mind and gotten her wish right. But she was pretty sure he was cheating her, and she'd never get to be rich and famous. Still, she had to be happy because she'd just saved the tribe from Zombiedom.

"Only the high priestess *knew* Farang had stolen the wizard's soul stone. She saw it all in a dream. So she waited, plotting her dark schemes. Some day, she would get Farang back. Some day!"

Brent grinned at the class. Julie flashed him a brief thumbs up. Maddy glanced at Kara, wondering if she'd noticed, but Kara was studying Brent with an expression of disgust. Ms. Mousumi's face was almost as pained.

"Thank you, Brent," she said. "You may sit down. Any comments?"

Kara's hand shot up. "What I don't get," she said emphatically, "is why Farang wouldn't wish to not be the pain eater anymore. It makes more sense that *that* would be her greatest wish."

Back in his seat, Brent shrugged. "Maybe it wasn't that big of a deal to her anymore. She got used to it. A chance at fame and riches was more important."

Kara rolled her eyes. Another hand went up. "How would Farang know about fame and riches, and toilets and Kleenex, and all that?" asked Nikki Nutter, a girl who sat in the rear row opposite Maddy. "She's lived in a tribe in a forest in, like, the stone age all her life. She's Neanderthal."

Brent grimaced, then shrugged again. "The zombies told her," he said. Snickers swept the class. Beside Maddy, Kara hissed, then started texting on her phone.

"How would the zombies know?" asked Nikki.

"Zombies," said Brent, "know everything."

"Actually," Harvir volunteered, "it was the wizard who talked about those things, not Farang."

"Oh yeah," said Brent, perking up. "And *he* would know – wizards know everything."

"Okay, okay," cut in Ms. Mousumi, getting to her feet. "We'll leave it there for today. Jeremy – you're up next, on Friday. No more zombies, though – the wizard is gone, so Zombiedom has officially been terminated."

Jeremy nodded. "Fine with me," he said.

"Glad to hear it," said Ms. Mousumi.

"Doo doo doo doo," someone sang softly.

Zombies, thought Maddy. That was what psychiatrists were for. And *she* wasn't a zombie. So she was never, never, *never* going to see a psychiatrist. Period.

The class moved on.

chapter seven

It was the Thursday lunch hour, and Maddy was hanging around the edges of the smoking crowd, listening in on conversations. Her usual smoking buddy, Jennifer Ebinger, was at a dental appointment, and so Maddy was at loose ends, drifting like an exhaled breath of smoke. Since no smoking was allowed on school property, students who had taken up the habit hung around the 7-Eleven across the street. Next to the store entrance, Jeremy was being chatted up by Julie. Jeremy wasn't a smoker – he played striker on the soccer team, and Maddy knew from Leanne that school policy stated that any sports team member caught smoking was to be cut, no exceptions. But Jeremy had friends who smoked, and on occasion he could be seen hanging out with them here, inhaling secondhand smoke.

Jeremy's *Pain Eater* chapter was due the following afternoon. Was Julie working her wiles, wondered Maddy as she watched the two – trying to *in-flu-ence* Jeremy? And if she was, would Jeremy go for it? He was well liked – not because of his appearance, which ranked about average, but for his easygoing personality and sense of humor. Which meant he didn't need the popularity boost Julie's approval could give him, but who knew? Popularity politics were twisted, the work of snaky minds with forked tongues. With a shrug, Maddy turned away. None of it was her business, and there were still seven surnames preceding hers on the class list. Anything could happen in the novel before her turn came up – a disease could wipe out half the tribe, the high priestess could shapeshift into a tarantula, or Farang could OD on the allura leaf poison and kick the bucket. Come to think of it, thought Maddy, she herself could come down with a near-fatal illness the day she had to read her chapter. She just had to plan her symptoms – a rasping cough and a lot of sniffing should do it. If she hyperventilated in her room before complaining to her mother, she might even be able to jack up her body temperature—

"Hey, Maddy," said a voice. Turning to face the speaker, Maddy saw a grade eleven student. *Herb Someone-Or-Other*, she thought. Whatever his last name was, the guy had never spoken to her before. Nondescript – a forearm tattoo, a phone in his shirt pocket – he was one of the stream of faces she passed daily in the halls. "So, you getting your daily nic dose?" he asked conversationally, leaning against a parked car. "Your nicotine vitamins?"

Maddy shrugged. The joke wasn't really worth a smile – kind of an insult to the intelligence.

"Nicotine make you happy?" asked Herb, studying her face. "Does it keep you smiling?"

Unable to make sense of what he was saying, Maddy frowned. What was the guy's point? And why was he talking to her? Was he a friend of Leanne's?

"What're you talking about?" she asked, trying to keep impatience out of her voice.

"Oh," said Herb, releasing a wispy smoke ring. "I'm just concerned about your happiness, Maddy. You don't look too happy these days. And it's important to keep happy, y'know."

Maddy stared outright, no longer bothering to hide her confusion. Stepping back, Herb gave her a silly little grin and saluted airily. "Have a good day, Maddy," he said. "A cheerful, *smiling* day."

He wandered off into the crowd. Face twisted in disbelief, Maddy watched him go. *What a weirdo*, she thought. Was he like that all the time, or did he have insanity attacks only during Thursday lunch hours? Exactly what she needed – some schizoid trying to randomly psych her out on her midday smoke break.

Or maybe not so random. When Maddy got to her locker to pick up her books for her afternoon classes, she found something small and white above her padlock – a decal of a Greek comedy mask, its broad grin leering at her. The glue on the back seemed to be extra-strength; no matter how she scratched, she couldn't get the sticker off. Nauseated and blinking back tears, she finally grabbed her books and took off down the hall, leaving the jaunty little sneer in place behind her.

• • •

He wasn't one of the five, Maddy was sure of it. Herb Whoever hadn't been one of the three who raped her, nor had he been the one to hold her down or the one to stand lookout. *He* hadn't been present in that copse of aspen last March in any capacity, but he knew about it. What exactly he knew, she didn't want to guess, but it was enough. And if he knew about it, so did others – outside the five guys directly involved and herself, that was.

It had to happen sometime, she'd known that – the story getting out, comments being dropped, smirks and stares. In a way, she was surprised it had taken this long. Although, when Maddy thought about it, Herb's comments had been pretty benign. There'd been no dirty innuendo, no sly nuance – just a keep-your-mouth-shut message delivered in a way that would make sense only to her. And even *she* hadn't gotten it until she'd seen the decal on her locker. If Herb or any of the five had finally decided to start leaking lurid stories about last March, they were going about it in a decidedly indirect manner.

She hadn't looked at her phone since the previous week's mask tweet, and she sure as hell wasn't checking it now. Instead, Maddy focused on just lying on her bed and keeping her breathing even. Her stomach ached; it felt as if she was digesting toxic waste instead of tonight's roast beef and mashed potatoes. She was probably getting an ulcer – she remembered her Aunt Cass talking about her own symptoms when she'd had one, and Maddy's current aches and pains fit the bill. That meant a diet of boiled vegetables, plain broiled chicken, and rice for months on end, she thought morosely. No Doritos, no french fries, no nothing that tasted like anything. Pressing both hands on her stomach, she swallowed a surge of bile. *This isn't an ulcer*, she told herself firmly. *It's just an upset stomach – something minor, like a bit of food poisoning.* If she didn't think about it, it would go away. What she should do was think about something else – something pleasant, something that would make her smile. When was the last time she'd laughed at anything? When had she last felt happy?

I'm just concerned about your happiness, Maddy. Casual, innocuous, Herb's voice floated through Maddy's mind. *It's important to keep happy, y'know. Have a cheerful, smiling day.*

Maddy lay, her face frozen, staring at the ceiling. Even here, in her bedroom, they had hold of her. They had hold of her face. If she smiled now, she was doing what they wanted, but if she never smiled at all, what did that leave her with? Were those her only two options – the two masks, one smiling, the other weeping? And either way – silence, never-ending?

Will anyone eat my pain? Maddy wondered.

• • •

Jeremy stood at the front of the class, studying the two pages in his hand. Beside Maddy, Kara thumbed her phone, an expression of calculated indifference on her face. As Jeremy had gotten to his feet, she'd quietly sung "Doo doo doo doo," but Jeremy had given no sign of hearing her.

Across the room, Julie was watching Jeremy, the usual smirk playing with her lips. Maddy's gaze flicked left, across David's, then Ken's, face. On cue, Ken's eyes leapt to meet hers, his expression so intense, Maddy felt it like something invisible coming at her. Dropping her own gaze, she started jamming in a thumbnail.

"I'm not sure if I got three hundred words," said Jeremy, glancing at Ms. Mousumi. "I was very tired when I finished writing this. I never knew sitting and writing something could wear you out." He took a deep breath. "When I was thinking about what everyone else wrote, I thought there was something missing. So I wrote about that. Here it is.

"Farang hated the full moon. Every month when it got close, she got scared and worried. Her stomach got upset so she couldn't eat. She couldn't fall asleep. Then, when she did, she got nightmares about a black monster that lived inside her and tore out her guts. She cried so hard she got headaches, and her eyes got blurry and she couldn't see much. Mostly, she curled into a ball and just stayed like that for days before the full moon.

"What was she scared of? Eating the poison, of course. Even if she didn't *know* the poison was there, every time she ate the food in the cage she *felt* pain. All of us feel pain. We know it's not great. But Farang's pain was monster pain. It was like an umbrella closed tight inside you that suddenly opens wide. It was like a tsunami way off in the distance – all the water sucked out, all the animals and humans run off to higher ground, and there's just Farang lying on the beach, because the tribe tied her up and left her there. So there she is all alone, waiting for all that pain to hit. Or it's like an electric drill, drilling into her gut. Or like lightning hitting from the inside out. Maybe it's the way cancer feels, when your cells are dying, and the life is going out of you bit by bit.

"But mostly I think it's like something coming awake inside of you. Something that isn't part of you, something like an alien that's gotten into you and hidden down deep, pretending to be sleeping, pretending to not be there – the way the moon gets small every month, goes down into almost nothing. Making you believe it's gone away and maybe won't come back. Because that was what the moon was to Farang. It was pain – pain that was horrible, pain that took over everything, pain she couldn't get away from by taking an aspirin. And most of all – *pain that wasn't hers*. And when it's not your pain, it's twice as bad. Ten times, a hundred times.

"That's the part of this story that I think is missing. The pain Farang has to face. The way it takes over everything, and really rips her to pieces every time. *Every single time*. And there's nothing she can do about it. There's that tsunami coming at her, and she's tied up alone on the beach, and everyone else has run away and left her, and she's going to feel it. We're just writing a story, but Farang has to feel it.

"I think we should all think about that a little more." In a dense, heartbeat silence, Jeremy walked to his desk and sat down. Three seats over, Maddy heard Paul Benitez heave a sigh. She shot Kara a glance to see the other girl sitting bolt upright, looking impressed. Julie's smirk, on the other hand, had wilted considerably.

"Well," said Ms. Mousumi. "I'm not surprised it wore you out to write that, Jeremy. You put a lot into it."

Jeremy nodded. "I guess," he said. "Feelings can be huge, y'know?"

The smile Ms. Mousumi gave him was brilliant. "So is genius," she said. "Class, this was a fascinating chapter that Jeremy's given us, but we're not going to have time for comments today. We have to complete our poetry unit, because Monday we start on some short stories. To do that, we'll be dividing into study groups, which I'll be naming off now. Group One: Kara Adovasio, Julie Armstrong, Emeka Kumalo, Amy Rupp. Group Two: Maddy Malone, August Zire, David Janklow, Vince Cardinal. Group Three…"

But Maddy was no longer listening. Her initial few seconds of curiosity, wondering how Kara and Julie were going to handle being within arm's reach of one another, had been smashed and scattered to the winds. According to Ms. Mousumi's list, she'd just been placed in a work group with David Janklow, one of The Masked Avengers…for days, maybe even for weeks. How on earth was she going to manage that? A leering mask tweet and a decal on her locker were bad enough, but this? She couldn't do it, there was just no way. Like Jeremy had said, feelings were huge. A thumbnail pressed into the back of a hand wasn't going to be enough to deal with it – she'd freak. She'd go crazy, psycho, and everyone would know.

Before she could stop it, Maddy's gaze lifted and flew across the room, directly to David's face. Mouth open, he was staring back at her with an expression of unmitigated horror.

Maddy's stomach imploded. A black monster awoke and began tearing at her gut. In her mind, she watched a vast ocean retreat into the distance, where it reared up, about to rush in on her. When it reached her, she would drown. She would drown in absolute terror. There was no way around it. There was just no way around any of it.

Maddy jabbed her thumbnail in so deep, she drew blood.

• • •

The classroom was emptying out. As soon as the bell had rung, Kara had leapt to her feet and clapped a hand onto Jeremy's shoulder. They'd left together, a society of mutual congratulations. Maddy hadn't watched David leave, or anyone else. She'd sat, a sodden lump in her desk, waiting until every other student had exited the room, then gotten shakily to her feet.

"Ms. Mousumi?" Slowly, Maddy approached the teacher, who was at her desk, keying something into a laptop.

"Yes, Maddy?" the teacher smiled.

"I was wondering…" Maddy's mouth had gone dry. Her tongue felt thick and oversized. She seemed to have lost the ability to think in words. "Well…" Suddenly, a sentence burst out of her mouth: "I want to switch study groups."

Ms. Mousumi's eyebrows rose. "For the short story unit?" she asked.

"Yes," said Maddy, her gaze dropping. Her heart was pounding so hard, it hurt. She felt like she was going to black out, drop in a faint straight to the floor.

Ms. Mousumi leaned back in her chair and studied Maddy. "Why do you want to switch groups?" she asked.

Maddy stood staring downward. She couldn't give her actual reason. She had no proof. And even if it was okay to say it without proof, the words were too enormous. It'd be like trying to shove a skyscraper out of her mouth. The reality of what had happened on that dark night last March just didn't fit into this sunny September afternoon classroom.

"Please," said Maddy. "It's important."

Ms. Mousumi sat silently. Maddy could feel the teacher's eyes probing her face. "I need a reason, Maddy," Ms. Mousumi said finally. "Part of the assignment is being able to work with classmates who aren't your personal friends. If you feel you can't work with someone in the group I've assigned you to, I need to know why."

"No, I can work with them," protested Maddy, her face growing hot. "I mean, most..." But she couldn't name David. To name him would result in further questions, each growing more specific. Just thinking about where this could lead brought on a wave of dizziness so intense, Maddy had to touch Ms. Mousumi's desk to remind herself where she was.

"Please," she said.

Ms. Mousumi took a careful breath. "You'll have to give me a reason," she said.

Despair took Maddy, whirled her around, and sped her toward the door. "Oh, forget it," she said over her shoulder. "Just forget I said anything." Veering too quickly around the back row of desks, she bumped the outer one. Pain tore through her right thigh, the shock of it blowing the last possibility of thought from her brain.

"Maddy, come back here," called Ms. Mousumi.

Putting on a burst of speed, Maddy made it out the door.

• • •

Terror lay inside her like a sickness. It pressed down on her like heavy sky. It wrapped around her like a cape; every time she turned, there it was – mocking, whispering, hissing. All weekend Maddy wore fear like a skin, seven layers deep, something so close it felt as if it had *become* her. Sitting alone in the tree house, she stared at the smudged mural opposite and struggled to keep calm, to keep memory dead and buried, where it belonged. A cigarette ember wasn't an option – she currently had five blisters in various stages of healing, and two looked to be infected. All five ached, and with the weather growing colder, she had to wear pants, which rubbed. To make things worse, the blisters were ugly. Maddy didn't like to look at them; their raw scabs and draining pus felt like something erupting out of her body – alien and evil. How had she become the person she was now? How had she gotten to this place of twisted self-hatred? *She* hadn't done anything wrong. *She* hadn't attacked and hurt someone else. So why was *she* being punished this way – shut out of ordinary human activity, all those normal parts of life like smiling, conversation, hellos and how are you's?

Despair reared up through Maddy, so absolute she could barely breathe. A pack of cigarettes lay within reach; she fumbled for it, then jerked her hand back. Not the fire. She *had* to stay clear of the blessed fire for a week at least. But how? The memories were awakening – she could feel them stirring in her gut. Soon they would be taking shape; they'd take over the inside of her head and then they'd rule. She would be back there again. It would happen again. It would be coming at her from inside, where there was no chance to get away. She had to stop it. She had to stop her head from letting the memories take over again. Her head was the problem – it was her *head*.

Maddy swung her head back against the tree house wall and felt a thud reverberate through her skull. Solid – the wall felt solid and strong, real. *Bam!* Again, Maddy swung her head back – not hard enough to hurt, just enough to keep her here in the real world, where she was alone, where she was safe. Again – *bam!* And *bam!* again, again. Each time, the thud took hold of her; it pulled her away from everything else; the thud was all there was and all there could be for as long as it lasted. *Bam! Bam! Bam!* A slow, steady rhythm, Maddy kept it up until nothing remained of the memories – they'd retreated back into her gut where they lived, waiting for the moment they could come at her again.

What she was left with was a dull nothingness in her brain. Her eyes felt glazed, her breathing was slow and even. If the back of her head now hurt, the rest of her did not. The rest of her, in fact, was ready for sleep – a sleep that could start immediately, a sleep that could go on, as far as Maddy was concerned, for the rest of her life.

Curling up on the floor, she sighed the sigh of the released and drifted off.

chapter eight

Monday afternoon, Maddy walked swiftly down the corridor toward her English class. She'd waited for the last minute; only the odd scurrying student could be seen as she reached the open door and the bell went off, pulling her nerves into high alert. Head down, she ducked through the doorway and to the right, averting her gaze from the desks to her immediate left, where Ken and David sat. If Ms. Mousumi glanced at her as she passed, Maddy didn't know it. Upon entering the classroom, she'd folded herself inward like a jackknife; her goal now was to be present as little as possible. From this point onward, during English class she would not exist.

If she didn't exist, her memories couldn't exist.

Maddy slid into her seat and focused on her left hand. To her right, Kara was talking animatedly with Jeremy, who'd turned around to face her. Then Ms. Mousumi began to speak, cutting through the chatter as she called the class to order. The student responsible for the next chapter, Elliot du Pont, ambled to the front of the room and stood momentarily surveying his phone.

Or so Maddy assumed. Since taking her seat, she hadn't glanced up and she didn't intend to ever again. From a distance, she knew Elliot as one of a lanky, wisecracking set of guys who usually took up position at the rear of a class and muttered nonstop jokes back and forth. The bane of a teacher's existence, Elliot draped himself in contempt as if it were the national flag. The only school club Maddy could envision him joining was the Science Club, and that would be in order to learn the more complicated interactions of acids and bases. As in acids and bases that led to explosions satisfying the cravings of the most avid anarchist.

"Okay," drawled Elliot, his voice meandering out of his mouth. "I didn't write much. To be honest, I think this is a dumb assignment. Or maybe the assignment is okay, but the story is dumb. Because we all know there's no such thing as a pain eater. You can't eat pain. How're you supposed to dine on it – with ketchup and mustard? Like I said, it's dumb. You can't eat your own pain, and you sure as hell can't eat someone else's.

"So that's all I've got to say about *The Pain Eater*. Pain eaters don't exist, so I can't write a story about one of them. End of chapter. Thank you and the end."

In the pause that followed, a few snickers trickled across the class. With a smug grin, Elliot began a laconic amble back to his desk. Wide-eyed, Maddy watched him progress to his seat.

Even for Elliot, the arrogance displayed here was surprising. It had caught Maddy off guard – so much so, she'd forgotten her fear and had watched him read his "chapter."

From her left came a sharp intake of breath. "What you have just observed, class," said Ms. Mousumi, rising to her feet, "is a student failing an assignment. Remember that you are each being graded on what you write, and that grade will contribute toward your final mark. Elliot has just earned himself a zero on this assignment – not for his opinion, but for his lack of effort. If you want to write a chapter about the tribe's misguided faith in pain-eating, fine. But work it into the story. Choose a member of the tribe and give him or her that opinion. And remember, the *minimum* requirement is three hundred words.

"Elliot, I will speak with you further after class."

Now seated, Elliot flushed but maintained his smirk. Curious as to the class's response, Maddy ran her gaze across the room, then jerked it to a halt and reversed. Empty – the desk in which David Janklow usually sat was empty. Disbelieving, she scanned the rest of the room, but he was nowhere to be seen.

"Okay, class," said Ms. Mousumi. "We will now be moving into our study groups. Shove your desks into groups of four, and I'll hand out the question guide."

Mayhem erupted as desks began scraping along the floor. To Maddy's relief, both Vince Cardinal and August Zire left their seats and came over to her, where they claimed Jeremy's and Kara's vacated desks. A fourth desk, which Vince also shoved into position, stood uninhabited, the empty space above the seat resonating with Maddy's relief. Unbelievable as it was

– *incredibly* – mercy had dropped down upon her world. It was a temporary reprieve; she knew terror would return next class, breathing once again down her neck, but for one day – one hour – she could breathe easy.

From several feet away, Maddy could feel Ms. Mousumi's gaze flicking across August, Vince, and herself, on the alert for signs of trouble. *Not today*, thought Maddy. No, today all was almost well with the world.

"Where's David?" asked Vince. "Is he sick?"

"I dunno," said August.

Maddy shrugged, a smile flickering across her face.

• • •

David didn't show up on Tuesday, either. As the bell rang, signaling the start of Wednesday's class, and his desk continued to sit empty, Maddy found herself settling into a confused wonder. How was it possible that David was missing class after class *just when she needed him to?* Was he ill? Had his family pulled him from school to go on some kind of trip? In grade six, she'd had a friend whose parents took her midterm to Kenya. Apparently the trip had been deemed "educational," and the school had allowed it. Was it possible David had left the continent on a similar educational experience? If so, Maddy hoped it was a world tour. She hoped his plane crashed in Siberia. Maybe terrorists would kidnap him. Maybe…

Dana Ferwerda walked to the front of the class, holding a tablet. "*The Pain Eater*," she announced, not quite catching Julie's eye. "Chapter ten. Well," she added, glancing at Ms.

Mousumi, "I didn't know if it was chapter nine or ten, because of Elliot. Does his count?"

Ms. Mousumi grimaced wryly, but didn't reply. "Well," Dana continued, "this is a real chapter, whatever number it is. Here goes. It was the full moon in September. The tribe was bringing in the harvest, and the hunters were working hard, killing animals for the winter. Everyone had a job to do. Everyone had to work hard and get things done, so the tribe could get through the winter.

"And then Farang went on strike. She had only one job to do for the tribe, and she had to do it only once a month at the full moon. All she had to do was eat one meal with the allura leaf in it. All she had to do was feel one stomachache, and then it was over. Then she was finished her job for the next whole month. She didn't have to work in the fields. She didn't have to sew or weave. She didn't have to hunt animals or skin them after. For the rest of the month – thirty whole days – she got free room and board and completely free time. She was free as a bird, except for one day when she had one job to do.

"And on the September full moon, she wouldn't do it. When the high priestess called her out of the bushes, Farang didn't crawl out as she always did. She didn't even walk out. No, she sat in a tree close to the clearing and watched what happened. When no one came out of the bushes, the high priestess called again. Still, Farang didn't come. So they sent out a search party, with everyone running around and searching. When they didn't find Farang, the high priestess called the temple priestesses together. There were five of them – the high priestess and four lesser ones. They all looked scared. Because they knew if Farang didn't eat everyone's pain, someone else had to. It was the law of the land, and they had to obey.

"The priestesses drew lots – the four lesser ones. The priestess who got the X cried out in dismay. She wept and tore her clothes. Then she crawled to the high priestess and knelt before her. Everyone in the village came up and gave her their pain. They hated doing it because this was the most popular priestess and everyone loved her. But the law was the law. After the priestess got everyone's pain, she crawled to the cage and ate the poisoned food. And then she died. She died a horrible death, twisting and screaming. Because, y'see, Farang had developed a tolerance to the allura leaf poison. The high priestess had only given her a bit at first, and slowly more and more. Because that's the way it is with some poisons – you can develop a tolerance for them. So the high priestess *had* to give Farang more and more, so she'd keep feeling pain. By this time, there was a lot of allura leaf poison in the bowl of food. A bit of allura leaf won't kill you. But the priestess had no tolerance for it, and since there was a lot, it killed her. She died, when Farang would've eaten the poison and gotten just a stomachache.

"When Farang saw this happen, she realized how selfish she was. She didn't know about the allura leaf because the high priestess never told her. But she did know she was strong enough to eat the tribe's pain, and no one else was. So she apologized to the tribe and went back to eating the poison. And they forgave her. Really, they should've executed her for murder, but the tribe forgave Farang and let her live.

"The end." Dana turned to face Ms. Mousumi. "I'll email you this at the end of class, okay?"

The teacher nodded, then stood as Dana returned to her seat. "Well, class," she said. "Any comments?"

Jeremy's hand shot up. "I think that's twisted," he said. "To say Farang just got a stomachache, as if it was, like, a bump on the head. Like I said in my chapter, she suffers – a lot."

"In *your* chapter," Dana said pointedly. "Not in mine. But either way, the priestess *died*. Farang killed her by not doing her duty."

"But the duty is wrong," broke in Kara. "It's not fair to make someone suffer like that. So Farang finally says no and stands up for herself. It's not *her* fault the priestess died. It's the high priestess's fault – she *knew* the food would kill the priestess who got the X, and she still gave it to her."

"How was the high priestess supposed to switch the food with everyone watching?" asked Dana. "She didn't plan to kill anyone. She expected Farang to eat it, and then everything would've been okay. It was Farang who caused all the problems by not doing what she was supposed to do."

"Still," said Harvir, leaning around Ken to look at Dana, "the high priestess *knew* it would kill the priestess, and she didn't do anything to stop it."

"What was she supposed to do?" snapped Dana, her voice rising.

Surprise crossed Harvir's face, and he settled back in his seat. "I dunno," he said diplomatically. "Just something."

A hand went up, and a quiet, careful voice began to speak.

"Excuse me," it said, "but I think we have two stories in progress, rather than one. Perhaps we need to take a vote, and decide which one we want to write."

"Perhaps, Sheng," said Ms. Mousumi, replying to the studious-looking girl who sat at the apex of the first row. "But perhaps that's the natural outcome of writing a collective novel – we're actually getting many mini-novels all compressed into one. I say we keep going the way we are. I'm certainly getting curious as to how it's all going to turn out. But now we have to move on, and get into our study groups for the rest of the period."

Desks shifted, and students migrated to their groups. August sat down beside Maddy, and Vince settled into the desk opposite August. "You're the one who gets the last word on all of this," he grinned at her. "Miss August Zire – how're you going to end it?"

August raised her eyebrows mysteriously. With her hair twisted into faux locs and large bangles dangling from her ears, she regularly turned heads. But she kept hers. This was the second year in which she'd successfully run for year rep to Student Council, and she also played tuba in the school band. "Wouldn't you like to know?" she cooed. "But I don't kick my dog, I can promise you that." Then her tone changed as she added, "Where's Janklow? Is he sick? This is the third day he's missed, and I'm tired of doing his work for him."

"He's skipping," said Vince. "My older brother works security at Midtown Plaza, and he told me he saw David hanging out at a video arcade nearby."

BETH GOOBIE

"Skipping!" burst out Maddy, shock lifting her out of her usual silence. "Are you sure?"

Vince gave her a startled glance. "She speaks!" he said. "She breathes! She's alive!"

"Lay off, Vince," August said, frowning. "She's shy. That's okay. At least she shows up and does her own work."

Maddy swallowed, trying to force the tremble out of her voice. She hadn't spoken more than the odd word since group work had started, but now she had to. She *had* to. "Why is David skipping?" she asked, her gaze not quite meeting Vince's.

"I dunno," shrugged Vince. "My brother saw him, not me. But it's not like David to skip. He studies hard, usually."

"I'd like to *slap* him pretty hard," muttered August, pulling out her laptop. "Slap him into next week."

"I'll call him tonight," said Vince, opening his binder. "Unless one of you wants to."

August hissed. Flushing, Maddy ducked her head.

"Okay," said Vince. "I'll call Janklow tonight and find out what's what."

• • •

So David Janklow was skipping. Her mind still reverberating with shock, Maddy sat staring at the smudged mural opposite. David was skipping, when he was a good student and didn't usually fool around – and this had all started exactly on the day he had to join a study group with *her*. Arms wrapped around her knees, Maddy sat still as still, working through the huge thoughts in her head. She recalled the look of horror on David's face last Friday as Ms. Mousumi had announced the names in Group Two. Her own fear had been so enormous, she hadn't thought about David's expression then, but now she replayed every detail in her memory.

David was afraid...*of her*. More than afraid, he was terrified – so terrified, he'd skipped three days of school rather than have to sit near her. Eyes narrowed, Maddy squinted at this fact, examining its meaning. She had been afraid too. She'd been scared absolutely shitless to face him. But she'd done it. Or rather, she would have if David had shown up. Terrified as Maddy Malone had been, she'd sucked it up and gone to class each and every day this past week.

Admittedly, this was because she hadn't known what else she could do. As far as she could see, there hadn't been any options. If *she'd* started skipping, her parents really would have made her see a psychiatrist. And there was no way Maddy was going to go anywhere near one of those. She was too full of ugly, black guck to let a psychiatrist poke around inside her, even just inside her thoughts. It hurt too much in there. It was full of moans and screams – moans she couldn't listen to herself, much less let anyone else hear.

So it hadn't been anything like courage – true grit – that had gotten her through English class these past few days. Still, she did have more guts than David. The realization resounded through Maddy like a note in a bell – a clear, full knowing. She had been able to do something David had fled from. Sure, she'd been shaking head to toe. Sure, Vince and August had ignored her like the bump on a log everyone assumed she was these days. But she hadn't run away. She hadn't skipped. No, she'd been there every day, staring at the empty seat across from her and pondering its implications.

David was more afraid of her than she was of him. Impossible as that might seem, it appeared to be true. Maddy took a deep, clear breath, then another. It felt so different – so *good* to be breathing air instead of fear. *I did it!* thought Maddy. *I did, and he didn't. He couldn't. Will he be able to tomorrow?*

Before crawling into bed that night, she took her phone out of her bedside table drawer and blocked @theneverknowns.

• • •

David was not in Thursday's class, and Vince admitted, shame-faced, that he'd forgotten to call. Annoyed, August sucked her teeth, and Vince promised he'd call that night. As Maddy sat opposite the empty desk David should have occupied, she felt almost as if she was pushing outward from herself, and taking up more space. She sat up straighter. Her brain pulled itself out of its usual dark fog. In her rear jeans pocket, she could feel her phone, now secure from unwelcome tweets. "No," she said at one point, breaking into a discussion Vince and August were having about the protagonist in the short story "War," by Timothy Findley. "That's not why he threw the stones at his dad. It was because—"

Her words were hesitant at first, and she stumbled, getting her thoughts out of her head. It had been so long since she'd done this – willingly participated in the give and take of real live conversation. Vince soon became impatient, cutting her off, but then August cut *him* off and made Maddy continue. In the end, it was Maddy's idea that was written down as the group answer.

So Maddy was flying as she made her way through the halls to her locker at the end of the day. Flying at half mast, maybe, in low-level sky, but still up off the ground. Even seeing the leering decal mask stuck to her locker wasn't enough to deflate her mood and bring her entirely back to earth. Until she saw what was beside it.

"What's this?" she muttered, studying it.

"It's from Maintenance," said Tim Bing, an older student from her homeroom who had the next locker. "They want you to get rid of that sticker."

That was obvious. The notice stuck to her locker read: *No decorations of any kind are allowed on the outside of a student locker. REMOVE IMMEDIATELY.*

"Crap!" muttered Maddy. "I already tried to get it off, but I can't."

"You didn't put it there?" asked Tim, hefting a knapsack onto his back.

"Uh uh," said Maddy. "And I don't know who did, either."

"Well," said Tim, "your best bet is probably a hair dryer."

"Won't that glue it on tighter?" asked Maddy.

"If you blow it on that sticker for *hours*," Tim grinned. "But a couple of minutes, and it'll just warm up the glue. Then the sticker'll come off easy. You'll need an extension cord, though. The nearest outlet is over there." He pointed to the baseboard opposite.

"Oh, double crap," said Maddy. "I guess I'll have to ask my dad."

"I have an extension cord I can bring tomorrow," offered Tim, closing his locker, "if you bring a hair dryer. Meet me here – say, eight-thirty – and we'll get it done."

"Sure!" said Maddy, a burst of radiance surprising her from within. "That's totally awesome of you. Thanks!"

Tim flushed, then turned to head off down the hall. "See you tomorrow," he said.

Maddy watched him disappear into the throng of students. Tim Bing – before this moment, she'd never spoken to him, other than the odd hello. And here he was, saving her butt from a potential run-in with Maintenance. Odd, how the world was so completely only one way – dark, heavy, the sky pressing down everywhere – and then it changed, lifting the sky back up to where it belonged, and letting you breathe normal air…breathe hope.

Hope. Maddy knew what it was that she hoped for. What she hoped was that David never came back. And that, wherever David was, Ken and the others joined him there. She hoped they all died and disappeared from the face of the earth – forever and ever, amen.

Closing her locker, Maddy glanced fleetingly at the mask decal. *Tomorrow you will be gone*, she thought. *I will destroy you, and you will be over.*

She started off down the hall.

chapter nine

David was there. He was there, sitting in his seat. Friday afternoon, as Maddy entered English class, the first place her eyes went was David's desk, and that was when she saw him, turned to his left and talking to Julie. Panic slammed her, and she veered right toward the front of the room and her own seat. It was over, she thought desperately. Her brief, four-day respite from terror was over. As Maddy sank into her seat, she broke into a cold sweat. Dropping her gaze, she started jamming in her thumbnail – grinding it in deep, *hard*.

Ms. Mousumi got to her feet. "Today's chapter will be given by Rhonda Hinkle," she said, interrupting the classroom chatter. "Rhonda, would you come up here, please?"

In spite of herself, Maddy glanced across the classroom, directly opposite, to where Rhonda sat at the end of the front row. Rhonda's reason for choosing this seat was obvious – born with cerebral palsy, she had limited mobility, and this was a relatively easy desk to get in and out of. Pushing herself up into a standing position, Rhonda took a moment to unsnap several pages from a binder. Then, in a slow, weaving motion, she made the brief, five-step journey to the front of the room. With a visible breath, she straightened her shoulders and threw her gaze straight out at the class.

"I can't," said Rhonda, her voice carrying clearly to every corner of the room. "All her life, Farang woke up and that was the first thing she thought – *I can't. I can't do what I want. I can't talk to anyone. I can't be happy. I can't be me.*

"Because *they* decided who I have to be. When I was born, my tribe decided who and what I was going to be in life. It didn't have anything to do with me personally. They could've chosen anyone to be the pain eater. But because I happened to be born when I was, it ended up being me. A fluke. Chance. Remember – if you were born to this tribe, it could've been you.

"What was it that got Farang thinking differently in her fifteenth year? What made her start waking up, thinking, *I can,* instead of *I can't?* Because she did – we know this from the first chapter. In her fifteenth year, Farang stopped believing she had to eat pain for the tribe. She stopped believing that they had the right to decide who she was and what she got to do in life. She stopped saying 'I can't,' and she started saying 'I can.' I can think for myself. I can be who I want to be. I can. *I can.*

"She knew she wouldn't get help from anyone else. If Farang was going to change her life, she was going to have to do it on her own. And, at least for now, she was going to have to keep it secret. So what she did was she built her own temple. Off in the woods where no one else went, she collected beautiful stones that she found by the river. They were only beautiful stones – each one a lovely color and polished smooth by the water. Some were of quartz, others had mica running through them, but they all had to make her feel as if lovely wings had opened inside her and were beating softly, lifting her up. Slowly, she built these stones into an altar. It wasn't an altar like the priestesses had in their temple, for animal sacrifices. Or where the high priestess put the soul stones sometimes, to put a hex on them. No, this was an altar for loveliness – for making life rather than taking it away. On this altar, there was no pain, only beauty and happiness. It was the place where Farang kept her soul.

"Or where she wanted to. Because her soul was trapped in a stone the high priestess had. So Farang knew she had to get the stone back from the high priestess. This was almost impossible, because Farang wasn't allowed in the temple unless she was with a priestess. She snuck in there alone at night, sometimes, but she'd never taken anything. And the high priestess kept a close watch on the soul stones – no one was allowed in her office except her. To take back her soul stone would be the hardest thing Farang had ever done, but she wanted to put *that* stone on the very top of her altar. So she made a vow to herself. 'I can,' she said, looking at the altar she'd built, with all its lovely, glowing stones. 'I can and I will.'

"The moon was on the wane that night, a half moon, so she didn't have to do any pain eating. While everyone else slept, Farang snuck into the temple and along the hall to the high priestess's office. Sometimes she saw a candle burning there, and then she knew the high priestess was hexing the soul stones. But tonight it was dark.

"Farang waited at the doorway, but she couldn't hear anything except the craziness of her own heart. Very, very quietly, she snuck across the room to where the stones were kept in a basket. She had a candle with her, to light her way. She started picking stones out of the basket and laying them on a table, so she could find her own soul stone.

"She knew she had to hurry. She knew the high priestess could put her to death for this. But she tried to forget about all that. She knew what her soul stone looked like – it was dark red, and the high priestess had dug jagged zigzag marks like lightning across it. Sometimes Farang could feel those lightning marks shooting through her body, as if the high priestess was digging them right into her skin. Then she knew the high priestess was drawing her finger across the marks in her soul stone, and sending a curse at her. So Farang knew what her stone looked like, and when she saw it in the basket, after she'd picked out about fifty other stones, she knew it right away.

"But it was too late. As Farang lifted her soul stone out of the basket, a shadow appeared in the doorway. It was the high priestess. Her face was white with anger, terrible to behold. 'What're you doing here?' she shouted. 'How dare you defile this temple by coming in here?'

"Farang felt fear like never before, but she held onto her soul stone. She stared straight at the high priestess and said, 'I can!'"

For a moment, Rhonda continued to stare fixedly at the pages in her hand, and then she lowered them. "I didn't write any more," she said. "This is already more than three hundred words. So I left what comes next for the next person."

A hand shot up. "Throw the stones, man!" Vince burst out. "Like the kid in 'War'!"

Laughter swept the class, releasing the tension Rhonda's chapter had built up. Ms. Mousumi laughed along with everyone else. "That," she said, when they'd quieted down, "will be up to David Janklow. I'm glad you've rejoined us, David – just on time for your chapter. You can catch up on the chapters you missed by checking the website. We'll hear from you on Monday. Now, everyone, we'll move into our study groups."

Desks began to move as students shoved them into new positions. August settled in beside Maddy; Vince reversed the two desks in the first row, and sat down facing August. As the two of them struck up a conversation, Maddy sat, shrunk into herself and riding the kick-ass thud of her heart. Her mouth had gone dry; her stomach felt as if it was melting down the inside of her legs. Directly opposite, the empty desk waited. Maddy couldn't think, couldn't *think*. It was about to happen – David was about to cross the room and sit down across from her, and it wasn't possible, it just wasn't possible to keep sitting there with one of *them* so close, so—

The blurred outline of a body appeared at the desk opposite, and Maddy felt a slight bump against her own desk as David sat down. "Nice of you to show up," commented August, but before David could reply, terror took hold of Maddy; it rose through her in an absolute wave that picked her up, lifted her out of her desk, and shoved her toward the nearest wall. There she stood, hugging herself and trembling. Thoughts tore every which way in her head; her heart thundered like a crazed thing; with a whimper, she turned her back to the class and pressed her face to the wall.

"Maddy?" A hand touched her shoulder. "Maddy, are you all right?"

It was August. Flinching, Maddy pulled away. "What's the matter, Maddy?" asked the other girl.

Beyond August's voice, Maddy could hear the ongoing chaos of desk-shoving and student chatter. The noise was reassuring; it moved in and wrapped around Maddy's fear like a cocoon, muffling and calming it. Cautiously, she turned to look at the class. Groups were still setting up; in a far corner, Ms. Mousumi's back could be seen as she stood talking to some students. Closer in, David sat slumped in the desk opposite her own empty one, staring downward. Turning his head, he said something to Vince. Then, as Maddy watched, the two boys stood and switched places.

"Will that help, Maddy?" asked August, concern creasing her face. "Are you scared of David? What's the matter with David?"

Wordless, Maddy stared at her empty desk. Her heartbeat had slowed, its thundering quieter. Besides her own study group, no one seemed to have noticed her sudden panic. Maybe if she got a grip, Maddy thought, she *could* sit down again. David wasn't going to jump her in a classroom packed with kids – this wasn't a night street with no one around, she was safe here. If she could somehow manage to sit down now, August would lay off, and everything would go back to being normal, to being what it was supposed to be.

"I'm fine," Maddy said, not looking at August. "Don't worry about it. I'll be okay."

"Are you sure?" asked August. "I can call Ms. Mousumi."

The teacher's back was still turned. Incredibly, in spite of her initial careful scrutiny of Maddy's work group, now that the crisis had occurred, Ms. Mousumi had missed it.

"No!" said Maddy. Forcing herself to move, she brushed past August and walked to her desk. She felt jittery all over – buzzed; as she sat down, she bumped her right knee hard. Once seated, she slumped into her usual position, head down, a mirror image of David, now sitting kitty-corner to her. Whatever his reason for moving there, she realized immediately, it helped. It helped a lot. Sitting at an angle to him was still too close, certainly, but at least they were no longer directly face to face. How had David known this would improve things? Taking a long, shuddery breath, Maddy tried to clear out her fear. Beside her, August sat down.

"Okay," said August. "Let's get this show on the road."

"You read 'War' last night like I told you?" asked Vince, turning to David.

"Yeah, I answered the questions you gave me," said David, and passed him some notes.

Vince read David's responses aloud, with August throwing in a few comments. Then the three began working on a group response to the question: "How does the protagonist's conflict with his father mirror the larger social milieu in the story 'War'?" Maddy contributed nothing. She had worked out her own answers the night before, but she didn't open her binder now, nor did she volunteer any comments. Simply sitting there and surviving her heartbeat was enough. While her out-and-out terror had retreated, her body remained in its own state of war, within touching distance of the enemy and on high alert.

The other three left her alone. As far as August and Vince were concerned, Maddy figured, she was a nutcase, a bump on a log best left undisturbed. She didn't blame them. They were both nice kids – didn't kick any dogs – but neither had volunteered to be friends with a freak, and as of today, Maddy definitely qualified. As for David, he obviously wanted as little to do with her as possible, which was fine with Maddy. In fact, as far as she was concerned, she wanted nothing to do with anyone. The present situation was fine with her – so fine, it was almost perfect.

When the final bell rang, she waited as the other three stood and walked away, then got to her feet and left the classroom.

• • •

Saturday, late afternoon, Maddy sat alone in the tree house, smoking and flipping through a photo album. A July birthday gift from her mother, it contained enlarged color prints of Maddy, from her birth into her fifteenth year. Delores Malone insisted on prints of all her favorite photographs, especially of her daughters. Electronic images didn't do it for her; she said they were only halfway to being real.

Smile after smile passed through Maddy's hands. There she was – in Halloween costumes, in a Girl Scout uniform, midway through an art project and smudged with paint. Or climbing out of a wave pool with friends. Posing in ballet shoes and softball uniform with Leanne. Pictures of herself with Leanne outnumbered those with anyone else; until a month ago, Maddy had thought of her older sister as an extension of herself – something to take for granted, like a hand or a foot.

Not anymore. These days, Leanne could barely stand to remain in the same room. As soon as dinner was over, she was up and out the door. Maddy couldn't remember the last time her sister had looked at her, spoken her name.

Or anyone else, except maybe her parents. And there was that moment yesterday, when she'd freaked and pressed her face to the wall, and August had tried to calm her down. *Take it easy, weirdo*, Maddy thought, wincing at the memory. *You're acting like a baboon, an orangutan. Get a grip and get yourself back to the human race.*

August hadn't said anything like that – she'd been really nice, in fact – but she must have been thinking it, thought Maddy. And no wonder, what with the way Maddy had been cringing against the wall, acting as if the world was about to end. What the hell was wrong with her, acting like that? David's sitting down across from her wasn't *that* big of a deal. He wasn't, after all, one of the three who'd raped her. Why couldn't she let go of the whole thing and get on with her life?

Slowly, Maddy scanned several more photo album pages – pictures from her grade eight Farewell Ceremony, in which she was wearing a powder blue dress and a corsage. As she stood with a group of girlfriends, her grin was ear to ear. Nothing in that moment could have predicted what was coming – there was no premonition, no foreshadowing of approaching doom and the changes it would bring – that moment in the trees when the-Maddy-who-was ended, and the-Maddy-who-was-now moved in to take her place.

That's it, she thought dully. *That part of me – the part that was before – is over and gone. Terminated.* Bitterness swarmed her. Lifting the cellophane sheet that covered the photographs, she removed a picture of herself in blue dress and corsage, and tore it end to end. The *riiiiip* was satisfying; as Maddy watched her smiling face split apart, anger leapt through her. That anger felt like coming awake – powerful and good. Finally, she wasn't a wimp, cringing against a wall. Finally, she was active, choosing, *doing* something.

Selecting another picture, Maddy tore it in half, then into quarters and eighths. Another picture followed, and another. Page emptied, she flipped to the next and ripped into the smiles and giggles she found there – hugs and family togetherness, what was lost and would never be regained. And why wouldn't it be regained? she thought in disgust. Because of *herself* – Maddy Malone. Because she'd been stupid. She'd been stupid enough to be out walking home alone in the dark when she should have known better. If she'd known better, none of this would have happened. It wouldn't have happened, and she'd still be the girl she was before – a girl who could smile, who could laugh as if she got happiness for free. *What a loser!* Maddy thought contemptuously. *What a freak! Bitch!*

Fragments of photographs lay scattered all around – faces split in half, bodies separated from heads. Tears streamed down Maddy's face; an odd growling came from her mouth. Looking up from the mess of her life, she focused on the smudged mural opposite. Without a clear thought in her head, she grabbed an old sweatshirt lying nearby and wiped until the wall was clean. Then, yanking open a box of chalks, she grabbed a stick of black and began rubbing it across the now-blank wall. Twisted shapes appeared under her hand – no, not even shapes, just darkness shifting, the way a groan would look if it could be seen. It had been over a month since Maddy had done any drawing, but now she felt it happening the way it did when her hands were about to show her something, when her soul leaned out of her body into the chalk and took over, so that the wall before her – and the chalk, her hand, her mind – all became one, pulling what was unformed and indescribable into the real world, where it could be seen, touched, known.

When she ran out of black chalk, Maddy picked up a brown and let it run itself through the black – swirling, shifting, *moaning* along the wall. Her breath came quick and fierce, her tongue caught between her teeth, her eyes intent. She could not have explained what she was sketching; the thoughts in her brain resembled the dark formlessness on the wall, but something deep and alive had risen within her; she could feel it pulsing through the chalk in her hand. When she ran out of brown, she moved on to gray – smudging, blurring, *gouging* the colors together. Finally, with the gray also down to a stub, she settled back onto her heels and surveyed what she'd drawn. Spent, she was utterly spent, her arms so heavy she couldn't lift them, and the wall ahead of her was a mass of black, brown, and gray – formlessness mumbling to itself. And yet it was a beginning – the beginning of what, she didn't know, just that it was leading somewhere, and wherever it went, she had to go with it.

Maddy slumped to the floor and lay there, listening to the beating of her heart.

chapter ten

David stood at the front of the class. His shoulders slumped and he kept his eyes fixed on his phone. Though Maddy hadn't worked up the courage to send him more than a single, skittering glance, it was enough to tell her that he was nervous. In fact, from the looks of things, nerves were eating David from the inside out.

At the back of the room, Julie and Dana wore expectant expressions. *Of course,* thought Maddy. David would be one of their prime *in-flu-ence* targets. And, sitting right smack dab next to Julie, he would probably be eager to stay on her good side.

"*The Pain Eater,*" croaked David, then flushed and cleared his throat. "Okay. Farang stood behind the basket of soul stones, staring at the high priestess. She had her own soul stone in her hand. She thought about throwing it at the high priestess and trying to make a run for it. But then she'd lose her soul again, and that's why she was here – to rescue it.

"So she swallowed her soul stone. It was a small stone and smooth, but not easy to swallow. It hurt going down, but it wasn't impossible. But it took concentration to swallow, so the high priestess had time to reach Farang and grab her so she couldn't get away. Then she dragged Farang out of her office and into the main part of the temple, like a sanctuary in a church, I guess. The high priestess was big – not fat, but tall and with lots of muscles, like an athlete.

"Once they were in the sanctuary, the high priestess screamed and pushed Farang around. 'Help! There's a thief in the temple!' She wanted Farang to be discovered, y'see, but not in her office, because she had secrets there. But the sanctuary was okay, so she kept screaming and hitting Farang, and acting like she'd found her there. Farang fought to get away. She didn't want to hurt the high priestess – just to get out of there.

"The other priestesses came running. There were three, now that the other one had died. They grabbed Farang and held her, to give the high priestess a break. Think about it – it was creepy in there. An old temple, with glowering statues of the gods and candlelight flickering away. And maybe an altar where they sacrificed animals, or maybe even humans. No sunlight, not even moonlight – just these four creepy priestesses crowded around Farang, all mad as hell because she'd managed to get her soul back.

"Well, no – just the high priestess knew *that*, but the other three were mad that she'd trespassed on temple grounds. That's a big sin in this tribe. So when the high priestess says Farang has a demon in her and they have to baptize her in the river right away to get it out, they all agree. They all grab Farang and drag her to the river. Farang kicks and fights. She knows a baptism in the middle of the night by four mad priestesses isn't going to be a high point in her life. But the tribe are all asleep. There's no one to see. And the priestesses are being quiet now. One has her hand over Farang's mouth so she can't cry out. They're at the riverbank, going into the water.

"But now there *is* someone watching. It's a boy, fifteen years old like Farang. He's not anyone in particular, just a kid who couldn't sleep and so he got up and walked around instead of lying there staring at the dark. So because he's up, he hears the noise and comes over. He doesn't want to be seen, so he stands behind a tree and watches."

David's voice faltered and he paused. "He doesn't know what to do. He sees the priestesses push Farang under the water and hold her there. At first, he thinks it must be a weird baptism, but they're holding her under so long. But they're priestesses, y'see, and priestesses are supposed to be good, and do what's right. And one of the priestesses is the boy's aunt. He knows her personally.

"But Farang has been under so long. The boy is holding his breath. He hasn't breathed since they pushed Farang under. And his own lungs are almost bursting – he can't help it, he *has* to breathe. And *still* they're holding Farang under.

"Finally, the priestesses let Farang come up. She isn't moving. They drag her to shore and dump her there. Then they spit on her and go back to the temple. The boy stands behind his tree, breathing and breathing. He can't get enough air into his lungs. He's never thought about breathing before, and now he thinks he'll never forget how important it is.

"He doesn't go to Farang. He's too afraid of the priestesses. He watches her. So he sees when she starts to move, and when she finally sits up he's so relieved, his legs give out and he has to sit down. But he stays there. He stays and watches, until he sees Farang crawl away from the river. Then he follows and sees her crawl into a safe place under a bush and go to sleep.

"He gets her some food and leaves it nearby, for when she wakes. Then he sits and watches while she sleeps. He isn't a hero, that's for sure. And he's not a bad guy, either. He *didn't* join in. He's just an average, ordinary kid who happened to be there when it happened. He saw it happen, he watched. Now he watches while Farang sleeps. When she wakes, he watches her eat. And when he knows she's okay, he goes away.

"He never tells anyone what he saw, but he knows. He's a watcher and a knower."

Silence hovered around the end of David's reading like a breath held in. David stood quietly, as if caught up in the tail end of his story. Equally quiet, Maddy sat trapped in the sledge-hammer thud of her heart. Every word that David had read in his hoarse, faltering voice felt as if he'd spoken it directly into her body. She felt as if she'd heard them *inside* herself. It had been exhausting. Glancing across the room, she saw Ken sitting with his dark eyes fixed on David. Nothing in Ken moved; he didn't appear to be breathing. Maddy's gaze flicked to David, who continued to stand silently, his head down.

A hand went up. "What is his name?" asked Emeka, a boy in the first row.

David's head jerked up, the color fleeing his face. "Huh?" he asked.

"His name," said Emeka. "The boy who is watching – what is his name? I need to know. I come next."

"Oh," said David, staring off into the middle distance. He seemed dazed. "I dunno. I didn't think of one."

"I guess you'll have to come up with one, Emeka," said Ms. Mousumi.

Dana's hand went up. "This boy," she said slowly, like a police investigator after the facts of a case. "He's not supposed to talk to Farang or help her. So why does he bring her food?"

David grimaced, as if confused. "Wouldn't you?" he said. "I mean, if you saw something like that happen?"

The hand that rose next was Christine's. "But Farang is *supposed* to feel pain," she said. "That's her job for the tribe. So pain is good when it happens to her, isn't it? At least, someone who lived in *this* tribe would think so, wouldn't he?"

"Maybe," said David, shifting foot to foot. "But Farang's supposed to get it on the full moon, and it's supposed to come after she eats a dish of food. It's not, like, open season, is it? Anyway, it's different being *told* the way things are supposed to be, and then suddenly you *see* something like that happening…" David's voice trailed off, and he stood once again staring into the middle distance.

Maddy's heart thundered in her throat. Her eyes were riveted to David's profile, Krazy-Glued to his face, awaiting his next words. But they didn't come.

"Well," said Ms. Mousumi, rising to her feet. "That was a very thoughtful chapter. Thank you, David. You may sit down. All right, class, we're moving on to the short story 'The Sniper' today. Get into your groups and I'll hand out the worksheets."

Desks began to move, but before Kara stood, she handed Maddy a folded note. "Give this to David," she said. "Okay?"

Without waiting for Maddy's response, she walked away, and Maddy watched her go, wondering how Kara felt about being doomed to another week of working with Julie. She didn't have much time to ponder this. Within seconds, August and Vince dropped into place, beside and across from her, and then David was edging himself onto the seat opposite August. Convulsively, Maddy shoved Kara's note at him and shrank back. David stared at the folded bit of paper as if it was about to attack him.

"Great chapter, David!" said August.

David gave a cautious smile. "Yeah?" he said, his eyes flicking across August's.

"I thought so, too," said Vince. "I could really see it happening. You're a good describer."

David's shoulders straightened, and he looked quietly astonished. "Thanks," he said, picking up the note. Fiddling with the edges, he started to open it, then jammed it into his shirt pocket.

"It's from Kara," blurted Maddy, her voice cracking.

"Oh," said David, his head jerking back. Taking the note from his pocket, he read it. A smile crossed his face, and he returned the note to his pocket.

"Kara liked it?" asked Vince.

"She liked it," David replied.

"The high priestess of English class approves," August said wryly.

"Uh uh," said Vince. "That's Julie. Haven't you heard how she and her priestesses are going around telling kids what they're supposed to write about?"

"Since when?" demanded August.

"I dunno since when exactly," said Vince. "They didn't talk to me, but Doody told me they were on his back. They talk to you?" he asked, turning to David.

David shrugged. "Julie sits beside me," he said. "That doesn't mean I obey her."

"Doody did," said Vince. "And Dana. And Christine. And probably Elliot, though with that guy, who knows."

"But not Jeremy or Rhonda," August pointed out. "If Julie's twisting arms, she didn't get anywhere with them. I dunno, Vince. I don't think Julie—"

"She is," Maddy broke in, the sound of her own voice so abrupt, it felt like a dinner plate breaking inside her head. Her heart leapt into high gear; her hands sweated. Keeping her eyes down, she forced words out into the astonished silence that greeted her. "I heard her and Dana talking in the can about... two weeks ago now." And she described the September eleventh encounter.

"Whoa!" said Vince, when she'd finished. "What'd I tell you?"

"Looks like," August admitted. "But Kara's doing pretty much the same thing, isn't she?"

A sudden surge of – Maddy didn't know what – washed over her. "Kara's not going around threatening people in the can!" she protested, flashing August a glance. To her surprise, the other girl smiled at her, white teeth brilliant against her dark skin.

"Hey, Maddy," August said softly. "You go, girl."

Maddy flushed and dropped her gaze. Kitty-corner from her, David shifted uneasily. "It's like an election, almost," he said. "Everyone's got their own opinion. But that's okay. You've got to let them talk the way they want to. Except," he added hastily, "they shouldn't be going after other kids in the can."

Even with her eyes glued to her lap, Maddy could feel David keeping his gaze carefully averted from her. Still, he was speaking directly *to* her, she knew that. Just like his entire chapter today had been a delicate gift laid open for her. There was no doubt in her mind – he had given it to her. He wanted her to know this: *I happened to be there. I didn't join in. I never told, but I know. I'm a watcher and a knower.*

Did *he* watch *her* after it happened, to make sure she got home safely? Maddy sat, pushing against the weight of her own silence. It was a great weight but she was almost past it, almost ready to look up and ask…and then August picked up her worksheet, Vince started to read the first question aloud, and the moment passed.

• • •

Maddy knelt in the tree house, watching the dark mural she'd begun on the south wall. *Watching* was the word for it, she thought, because if she kept herself still for long enough, parts of the mural began to move. At first glance, she saw only formlessness – charcoal and chestnut brown smudges that overlapped. But if she let her eyes go vague, almost out of focus, she could feel the colors begin to shift, drift into each other, *groan*.

The groans didn't frighten her. As she watched, her heart thudded slow and steady; she felt something dark and unnamed shift deep within herself. That inner shifting and what she'd drawn on the wall seemed to go together; Maddy could feel the formlessness inside herself reaching out toward the wall, as if wanting to connect. She thought of Rhonda Hinkle standing before the class and proclaiming "I can!" She thought of David, his head down, saying, "Just an average, ordinary kid. A watcher and a knower." Well, that was what she was too – an average, ordinary kid now staring at some kind of knowing…a knowing that was undefined, something inside herself that wanted out.

I can, Maddy thought. Poking through a box of chalks, she chose a cream-colored stick and began to work it into the dark formlessness twisting across the wall. No words spoke in her head; no image presented itself – she knew nothing about what she was drawing, and yet a knowing *was* with her – she felt she was at the beginning of everything. *I can*, she thought again, her hand trembling as it picked up a pale yellow. *This is mine, whatever it is*. Silently, she continued to work, watching the colors blend, the yellow lose itself into the darkness around it. *Almost as if it never was*, she thought. *There's so much dark*. And yet where she continued to work the yellow chalk, the darkness lightened somewhat, a pale presence there within the gloom.

Higher, something in her said. *Go higher*. Raising her hand, Maddy began to work farther up on the wall, in cream and gold and slight smudges of orange – a sphere that hovered above the lower darkness. After a while, she settled back on her heels and regarded the fuzzy blur she'd created. If asked, she couldn't have said what it was meant to be, but it held part of her – she knew that much. And it gave her satisfaction, as if drawing this sphere had in some way made her more solid, had given her a stronger standing in the world.

She and this wall had a long conversation ahead of them. Maddy could still hear its groaning. And the wall seemed to be able to hear and receive hers. It was a beginning – enough to make her keep going.

• • •

Emeka smiled apologetically at the class. Tall, with glasses and shortly cropped hair, he wore his usual polite, wary expression. "I am sorry," he said, in carefully enunciated English. "My English is not excellent. But I will do my best."

Wednesday afternoon, Maddy sat slanting glances across the classroom at David. Head down, he'd positioned himself at an angle in his seat, so that he was leaning visibly away from Ken. Rigid and upright, Ken looked grim.

Beside Maddy, Kara's desk sat vacant. Accustomed to the other girl's presence, Maddy felt exposed, as if part of her defence system was missing. A cluster of thumbnail welts rode her left hand.

"I think," said Emeka, "we must talk about tribes. What is

a tribe? There are black tribes and white tribes, so that does not matter. Tribes are about family, and people who live together stay alive in the jungle. Not like we live here, where people live separate without troubles.

"So in Farang's tribe, everyone must be together. Together, they make food to eat. Together, they make warm clothes, and houses and fire. Together, they believe in the same gods. It is so, *so* different from here, where we believe different things. In a tribe, everyone thinks the same. They think the same to *live*. You cannot think, *Oh, I will believe this or that, whatever I want.* You obey your parents. *They* think, *you* think. *They* say, *you* do. Or the tribe says, 'Go away now.' You are alone and you die.

"Farang has her beautiful altar in the forest. It is her secret. She does not tell anyone. And she swallows her soul stone and gets her soul back. Only she and the high priestess know that. But she cannot go away from the tribe. She must think like them and do what they say. Or she dies. That is life in a tribe. It is tradition. Even in a tribe in a story that is how it is.

"And one more thing. Kara said a pain eater comes once in a generation. A generation is ten, twenty years. Farang is fifteen, so a new child must come soon. What happens to Farang? She will die then. She will die to make a place for the new pain eater. Maybe in a year, or in two or three. But she will die. Yes, she will die.

"Thank you." With a polite nod, Emeka started for his seat, but Ms. Mousumi called him back.

"Does anyone have a comment for Emeka?" she asked, getting to her feet. All over the room, hands shot up.

"There are always people who think different in any group," said Rhonda. "Everyone all over the planet started out in tribes, but things changed. People thought differently and they changed things, and now we don't live in the stone age anymore."

"Emeka?" asked Ms. Mousumi.

"You are thinking from the way you live here," Emeka replied. "In Farang's tribe, there is no thinking different. It is all the same. Tradition. No Internet, no phones. No books. Where does different thinking come from for them?"

"Jeremy?" asked Ms. Mousumi.

"The rebel," said Jeremy. "There's always a rebel in every group. Someone who thinks just a little different."

"Like Galileo," said Theresa.

"Gandhi," called Harvir.

"Princess Di," said August, raising a fist.

"Yes, Amy?" said Ms. Mousumi, pointing to a girl who sat next to Jeremy.

"I heard of a Doctor Semmelweis," said Amy. "He invented germs, sort of. Or figured out they exist. It was in the eighteen hundreds. He started telling other doctors to wash their hands before they did operations or delivered babies, because he said germs caused infections and people died from them. And people said he was crazy, because they couldn't see the germs, of course, and they took away his doctor's license. But he kept going on about it, so in the end they put him in an insane asylum and he died there."

The class sat, silenced by this information. Amy flushed.

"That was in Vienna," she added. "Not a tribe, I guess. But he thought differently, and look what happened to him."

Emeka nodded. "So, you see, it happens in Vienna too," he said. "In Farang's tribe, it is even more like that."

August's hand went up. "But isn't the real point that it changed *eventually?*" she asked. "And that the doctor stuck to what he thought, even if he got put in a loony bin for it? You're gonna get creative thinkers anywhere and everywhere, even in a tribe like Farang's."

"I am saying don't forget tradition," said Emeka. "In a tribe, tradition is strongest. It is the way it is."

"Thank you, Emeka," said Ms. Mousumi. "I think we'll leave it there for today. Sean Longstreet, we'll hear from you on Friday. Group time, everyone."

Maddy sat rigid, still braced against what hadn't come. Next on the class list, after Longstreet, came Malone – she was sure of it. She'd gone over everyone's surnames in her head, and the inevitable had arrived – her chapter was due next Monday. But by fluke or by luck, Ms. Mousumi hadn't called out her name, which meant it wasn't *quite* inevitable yet. At least, that was the way Maddy decided to think about it.

Vince and August, then David, drew up desks and sat down. Hesitantly, Maddy shot David a glance. Yesterday, he'd been cautious, never looking at her directly and speaking only to Vince, but fully planted in his seat. Today he was back to leaning as far away from Maddy as possible – so far his butt hung halfway off the seat and was hovering midair. Such intense unease radiated from him that Maddy felt swarmed by it. When she glanced across the room to Ken's group, she saw him sitting bolt upright in his desk, watching David.

Maddy's gaze dropped. Savagely, she went to work with her thumbnail, driving it in deep and using the pain to shove away panic and the thoughts that swarmed with it. She wasn't going to think about any of that now. In fact, she wasn't going to think about anything at all. Not about David, not about tribes and free thinkers, not about Liam O'Flaherty's short story "The Sniper." All she was going to concentrate on were the thin wedges of pain in the back of her hand, those tiny hot lines that kept everything else at bay. *Shit* – she'd broken through the skin and drawn blood. But blood could be good – it sharpened pain, and then there was nothing but pain…no thoughts, no fear.

Digging a Kleenex out of her pocket, Maddy pressed it against the small cut, pressed hard, *harder*. Pain pulsed, pulsed deeper, faded finally into numbness, and then Maddy was where she wanted to be – where there was no fear, there was no joy, there were no feelings of any sort – just a bump on a log, like everyone expected her to be.

chapter eleven

Thursday afternoon's English class was much the same – Kara
was still absent and, once the class had moved into work groups,
David again hovered half on and half off his desk seat, grunting
the odd reply. Frustrated at his lack of participation, August
snapped at him, but she didn't go after Maddy, who continued
to hunch, bump-on-a-log-like, without speaking. August, in
fact, seemed to have claimed some sort of protective status over
Maddy – though neither of them referred to it, Maddy could
feel the other girl standing guard. Vince, at one point, said, "Ask
Maddy, why don't you?" and August simply shook her head at
him. Vince got her drift – he left Maddy to bump along on her
log without interference from him, from anyone at all.

And so Maddy wasn't ready for it, she just wasn't ready
when, coming home from school, they jumped her again. It
wasn't that she'd thought it was over, but there had been nothing

since the sticker on her locker two weeks previous. So when she heard the sound of bike tires behind her in the alley, she didn't immediately take off. Instead, she turned to look, shading her eyes against the sun, and that gave them enough time to get close. She recognized Pete Gwirtzman first and whirled to run, but he ditched his bike and was on her, slamming her into a backyard fence. The wooden boards reverberated, giving off odd, muffled cries; soundless, Maddy cringed against them, one arm up over her face.

"Got her," said Pete over his shoulder, as footsteps approached. Desperately, Maddy pushed at him to get away, but he shouldered her back against the fence.

"Watch it, bitch," said a second voice – Robbie Nabigon, she knew without looking. "Where d'you think you're goin'?"

"Nowhere," sneered Pete. "Not until we say so. Got that, Mad-Mad-Maddikins?"

Wincing at the use of her family's nickname, Maddy remained silent. Head down, she kept her eyes squeezed shut.

"So, Maddy," said a third voice, and Maddy's eyes flew open. Ken Soong – it was him, standing directly in front of her. Maddy closed her eyes again. "Peekaboo, I see you," he said, his tone mocking, and Pete and Robbie snickered. "I'm still here, Maddy. You can't see me, but I can see you."

A hand shot out, grabbed her left breast and twisted it. Pain flashed through Maddy and she cried out. The hand let go. Maddy crossed both arms over her chest.

"What happened to the sticker we put on your locker?" asked Pete.

Maddy slitted her eyes open. The three boys were crowded close, leaning in on her, breathing open-mouthed. "Maintenance made me take it off," she mumbled.

"Fuck Maintenance!" said Pete. "We put it on there, it stays there."

"We don't want to get into trouble with Maintenance," said Ken. "Think of something else."

"Her shoes," said Pete. All three stared at Maddy's scuffed runners.

"Nah," said Robbie. "She'll get new ones soon. And you don't wear the same shoes every day."

"School notes," said Ken. "How d'you carry them?"

"A binder," croaked Maddy.

"Okay," said Ken. "Here's the deal." He grabbed her left hand and jabbed a smiling mask decal into it. "Stick this on your binder," he ordered. "Right where you'll see it all the time. Everywhere you go at school, I want to see you carrying it. A reminder to keep your mouth shut. And keep smiling. Give us a happy face, Maddy. A *happy* face. And remember – don't tell anyone. *Don't* talk to David Janklow. Got it?"

"Yes," whispered Maddy.

"Yessie, yes, yes," Pete leered. "With you it's yes all the way."

And then all three were running for their bikes, pulling them up and taking off down the alley, whooping and hollering. Arms crossed over her chest, Maddy watched them go. Once they'd vanished around a corner, she picked up her knapsack, slipped the decal inside, and continued on home.

• • •

Maddy sat huddled in her desk, trying to keep her stomach down. In front of her lay her binder, the smiling mask decal stuck in a top corner. To her right, Kara's seat was once again empty. At midmorning break, Maddy had heard the rumor dominating that day's student information circuits – Kara's older brother, away at university, had committed suicide. By early afternoon, this had become established fact: two days ago, Frank Adovasio had shot himself in the mouth, and Kara would be away from school for a week, until after the funeral.

The class was in intense gossip mode, the air abuzz with chatter. At the front of the room, an unfamiliar woman sat at Ms. Mousumi's desk, frowning down at a lesson plan binder. Maddy hadn't yet glanced across the room to assess Ken's mood. When she'd entered the classroom, she'd been hit by tunnel vision. As she'd scurried to her seat, all she'd been able to see was the small circle of floor around her feet. Collapsing into her desk, she had concentrated on surviving her heartbeat.

The substitute teacher got to her feet. Calling for attention, she said, "Good morning. Your regular teacher is ill today, and I'm taking her place. I'm Ms. Wert. I understand you're working in study groups. How about you move into—"

A hand went up. "Excuse me," Sheng Yoo said politely, "but Sean has to read his chapter in our collective novel."

Seated in the back row beside Elliot du Pont, Sean grimaced and slouched farther under his desk. Ms. Wert gave Sheng a confused look. Several more hands went up. Theresa

Pronk explained, and Sean ambled reluctantly to the front of the class.

"*The Pain Eater*," he said, grimacing again. "Geez, y'know – Kara started this whole thing. If I'd a known last night.... Well, here goes. Everything that goes up must come down. And everything that goes in must come out. Farang swallowed her soul stone, and sooner or later it had to..." Sean grinned slightly, then added, "...return to the world." Snickers erupted, and Sean bowed. "The high priestess knew this, and so she locked Farang up in a cage – it was the cage she went into to eat the poison on full moons.

"Farang knew even better than the high priestess that the stone had to come out. She could feel it coming down the line – pain in her butt as it scraped along. The stone wasn't big but it was hard, and it hurt. And there was no doubt about it – she was going to lose it again, and there was nothing she could do about it.

"It usually takes about three days for you to...uh, get rid of what you eat, unless you ate too many grapes. So, for three days the high priestess kept Farang in that cage and didn't give her anything to eat. She made her poop in a bucket, and took that away and checked it for the stone. On the third day, the stone came out. Farang knew because it hurt like hell. The high priestess was waiting, and she grabbed the bucket. She took it to her office, cleaned off the stone, and put it in her best hiding place. After all the trouble she had getting it back, she wasn't letting Farang get at it again.

"After that, the high priestess let Farang out of the cage.

She had her soul back, so she didn't bother with any more punishment. She was the boss, she had all the power, and Farang had none. Like Emeka said, that's the way a tribe works. Farang crawled out of the cage. She ate the food a priestess brought her – it was just gruel, but it didn't have any poison. Then she wandered off to her secret altar. She laid down in front of it and cried. Her soul stone was captured again. She was back to square one. Life's a bitch, and then you die. Or should I say, life's a *shit* and then you die. Nothing ever changes. The end."

He turned to Ms. Wert. "I can email you an e-version after class, okay?"

Again, Ms. Wert looked confused. She also looked as if she wanted to forget what she'd just heard and move on to something else as quickly as possible. "Okay," she said.

Sean ambled back to his desk, and exchanged smirks with Elliot. Still huddled in her seat, Maddy didn't bother to check out Julie's expression for its approval rating. The moment of doom was fast approaching, and she was bracing herself for it. As Ms. Wert got to her feet, a conversation buzz started up all over the class, but it didn't appear to be a response to Sean's chapter; rather, students seemed to be discussing Kara and her brother Frank. Ms. Wert called out over the buzz, asking the class to move into their work groups, and they complied, the noise level rising dramatically as desks scraped along the floor. Still, no one approached the substitute teacher to correct her on her omission regarding *The Pain Eater*'s next chapter. In a state somewhere between shock and cataclysmic relief, Maddy watched the gossiping class forget all about Farang of Faraway as they chattered their way into various work groups. August's hesitation before settling into Kara's vacant desk was marked. David slunk into his seat opposite August, zeroed in on the mask decal on Maddy's binder, and blanched visibly. His gaze met Maddy's and ricocheted away.

As the class chatter settled to a low roar, Maddy saw Ken leave his work group and approach the teacher's desk. He smiled and began speaking at length, as if explaining something. Ms. Wert's face brightened, and she glanced in the direction he was pointing. Ken then returned to his work group, and the substitute teacher walked over to Nikki Nutter, the student Ken had pointed out.

Maddy almost dissolved onto the floor. Nutter was the surname following hers on the class list. Ms. Wert had to be talking to Nikki about writing the next *Pain Eater* chapter, which meant Maddy was off the hook, at least temporarily. And, due to the distraction of the news about Kara, no one appeared to have noticed. Impossible as it might seem, doom had passed Maddy by. Sure, it had come about due to Ken's intervention, but so what? Silence and obscurity were fine with Maddy; in fact, they were what she wanted most. Like Farang, all she wanted was to crawl alone into the forest and lick her wounds. Her soul had been stolen. Others ruled the world. Nothing ever changed. End of chapter, end of story.

Another thumbnail welt dug itself deep into the back of her left hand.

• • •

It was Saturday night. Alone in the tree house, Maddy sat observing the dark mural. Still in its earliest stage, barely defined shapes lurked and lunged at one another; above them hovered the faint cream-gold sphere she'd added earlier in the week. On the inside of her left thigh was a much smaller sphere that she'd burned into place Thursday after the assault in the alley. Since then, no further threats had been forthcoming – no more decals on her locker, no comments in the halls, no tweets. No nothing.

Her parents were watching a movie. They'd asked Maddy to join them, but she'd refused. Leanne was out with friends. *And here*, thought Maddy, *sit I – alone in Limbo Land. Depressed and unhappy. A fuck-up. A total, complete fuck-up.*

She wanted to be over this. She wanted to ditch this crap and get back to being part of the normal, functioning world again. Why wouldn't the pain just get over itself, go away, and let her get on with things? *Why? Why? Why?*

Maddy shifted the flashlight that she'd propped on several books so it lay tilted upward, its beam directed at the mural. Early October evenings were dark, and she was wearing a thick sweater – protection against the cold, keeping herself warm and safe…*for what?* she thought bitterly. What did it matter if she was healthy and alive? What was she continuing on for? She was just a smudge of nothingness these days – a blur of silence that everyone ignored. And why not? She was hardly worth paying attention to. She was a zombie. Her soul had been stolen, and it didn't look like she'd ever get it back. Why didn't she get a gun and shoot off her head like Kara's brother?

On the mural opposite, something moved. Confused, not sure what she'd seen, Maddy stared intently but saw nothing except the dark, tormented shapes she'd created. Nothing but her own nothingness. But then it came again – a kind of pulsing, there and gone. Breath in her throat, Maddy held absolutely still and watched. And yes, after a moment, she saw it more clearly – a shift in the darkness, something deeper down, darker still, reaching up toward the surface of what she'd drawn and making itself known to her.

I'm here, it was saying. *I'm here and I want you to know me.*

A tingling shot through Maddy; she felt herself coming slow-alive and on the edge of something. Picking up a stick of black chalk, she touched it to the place she'd seen the pulse surface. Then she began to sketch in quick, upward thrusts, pulling the deeper darkness up and out – a thick trunk of it that scattered itself outward into countless terrified branches. When it was done, she settled onto her heels and examined every inch of what she'd drawn – what she'd pulled up and out of herself and placed on a wall to be seen and identified like any other fact…the first tree.

Tears pricked Maddy's eyes. She blinked them back. *Not now*, she thought – she didn't have time to cry now. Not with the pulsing she felt deep within herself, a pulsing that wanted her heart and hands, that wanted out onto that wall. Later, she would cry. Now, she had work to do.

She started on the second tree.

• • •

Monday afternoon, Kara's desk continued to yawn empty. Ms. Mousumi was also once again absent, Ms. Wert sitting a little more confidently in her place. At the substitute teacher's cue, Nikki Nutter rose from her seat beside Sean Longstreet and walked to the front of the room. Openly curious, Maddy watched the other girl come to a halt and tap something into her phone. While no one would have guessed it from the current look of things, she and Nikki shared a history that went back to grade eight. They'd been friends then, smoked their first cigarette together, and played hooky a few times to visit video arcades. But Maddy had an older sister who kept an eagle eye on her life, someone who ran with the cool crowd but also talked sense. "Maddikins," Leanne had said. "D'you want to spend your life stocking shelves in a drug store?" Maddy had gotten her drift. Nikki, on the other hand, had no guardian angels. When Maddy had refused to skip any more classes, Nikki had dumped her and found other kids to hang out with. Nowadays, these included guys like Sean and Elliot. Nowadays, Nikki bleached her hair, wore imitation black leather, and sported lip and cheek studs.

Glancing at Elliot, Nikki winked. Then, her voice in a smoky drawl, she began. "Once upon a time in a land called Faraway, there lived a girl named Farang. When she was born, she lucked out and got a bum deal on destiny. Nothing went her way. Life was a bowl of lemons. No one loved her. It looked like she was always going to be everyone's kicking bag.

"So one day she sat down beside her secret altar and thought. And she thought and she thought. And she decided to make a change on her own. Y'see, the allura leaf wasn't the only poison the tribe knew about. There were good poisons too. Poisons you could drink. Poisons you could smoke. But make sure you inhale, to get all the fun! Farang knew where people in the tribe went to get these poisons. There was an old hag who gathered the plants, and dried and pounded them to powder, and sold them. Sometimes the people who bought them met by the river and partied. Farang started hanging around these parties. When the partiers got high, they forgot they weren't allowed to talk to her. They gave her powder to snort, and Farang got high with them. And then," – here, Nikki stopped and smiled knowingly – "things happened.

"Farang was ugly and she was lonely, and she was willing. *Very* willing. Farang was pretty much willing to do it with anyone. The sad thing was no one bothered to tell Farang the facts of life. So she got knocked up. She didn't know she was knocked up. She thought she was getting fat. She just kept partying and having a good time, and getting bigger and bigger.

"But the high priestess wasn't too pleased. Farang had disobeyed the rules of the tribe by going to the parties, and so had the partiers. She couldn't punish everyone who'd been there, but she could go after Farang. One full moon, the high priestess added a new poison to Farang's usual one. This was a poison that caused abortions. Farang didn't know she was eating it, because she didn't even know she was pregnant. The pain she went through that night was ten times worse than before. Everyone watched her scream and twist. They saw the dead baby come out. There was a lot of blood, and Farang almost died.

"The partiers got the message. They liked Farang – she was easy and always ready for a good time. But there are good poisons and bad poisons. The partiers knew enough not to eat anything the high priestess dished out, but what if she snuck into their huts and mixed something into their Frosted Flakes – or whatever they ate when they got the munchies. They chilled out on Farang after that. No matter how she begged, no poison and no nookie. So Farang was on her own again.

"What's the moral of this story? Everyone wants the good poisons. They pretend they don't, but they really do. Farang was like everyone else, except lonelier. So she wanted the good poisons more. When you're that hungry, you'll eat whatever you're fed. Farang lost her baby and her party friends, which made her very, *very* hungry. She was ready to eat anything. And so she began to look forward to the full moon when she ate the tribe's pain. At least *then* she got attention. At least *then* she felt full. It was her favorite time of the month; it was the closest to love that she got. Twisted, I know. But that's what life is – twisted. You better get used to it. Farang got used to it. In fact, she got to love it. She got to love pain, because it was better than hating it."

Nikki didn't look up when she finished her chapter. She simply shut off her phone, walked to her seat, and sat down. Sean leaned over and whispered something, and she smirked in reply, but there was no hiding the flush that was taking over her face. As Maddy watched her former friend, confusion took over her own face. *Twisted* – just like with Julie's chapter, this was the right word to describe Nikki's, but it was also the word to describe the expression on Nikki's face. She looked to be half laughing and, at the same time, half ready to cry. What had she been up to in the year and a half since she and Maddy had last spoken? What were Nikki's good poisons?

Maddy's eyes dropped to the smiling mask decal on her binder, then dove past it to her hands in her lap. Whatever was twisting Nikki's gut, she didn't want to know. She had enough of her own pain to eat, and she wasn't hungry for more.

"I think we'll move straight into your work groups now," Ms. Wert said briskly, getting to her feet.

Ms. Wert didn't want to know what was twisting Nikki's gut either. Neither did the rest of the class, now surging to their feet and shoving desks into new positions. For a moment, Nikki sat motionless, watching everyone move on to the next activity, purposely putting her chapter behind them as if they'd never heard it. The small smile playing on her lips said this was pretty much exactly what she'd expected.

chapter twelve

"Maddy, what the *hell* is going on?"

In the middle of chopping celery for a supper salad, Maddy turned to see Leanne standing in the back door. Beside Maddy, at the stove, Ms. Malone stopped stirring the spaghetti sauce. "What's the matter?" she asked her older daughter.

"I was just in the tree house," Leanne burst out. "The mural Maddy drew last summer – the scene of us having a picnic and the sunflowers – all of it's gone. Now it's a black mess – just a bunch of ugly black stuff."

Ian Malone came into the kitchen from the living room and stood leaning against the doorframe. As three pairs of eyes focused in on her, Maddy turned her back, thinking she would return to chopping celery. But a tsunami of panic kept washing through her, making her arms go limp. She set down the knife.

"Maddy?" her father asked softly.

Maddy stared at a closed cupboard door inches from her face. These people loved her. They loved every breath that went into her, and every breath that came out again. They would do anything in their power to keep her from harm, to help her in any way they could. Until half a year ago, they had thought they knew her. Until half a year ago, Maddy had thought she knew herself.

"It's just something I'm doing," she said. "It's a kind of experiment."

"It's creepy," Leanne said flatly. "Psycho."

"I'm not crazy!" cried Maddy, whirling to face her sister. Suddenly and entirely without warning, her blood was pounding, her fists clenched. Eyes widening, Leanne stepped back.

"I didn't say crazy," she blustered.

"You said psycho," said Maddy.

"Sorry," said Leanne.

No one moved, the silence dense, loaded.

"How 'bout I go take a look at it," Ian Malone suggested finally.

"No!" cried Maddy, taking a step toward the back door as if to block it. Again, silence took over the room, a breath sucked in.

"It's just..." Maddy faltered. "Please." She put both hands over her face. "It's just something I have to do. I'm looking for something, I think this will help me find it. It's not drugs or drinking, it's nothing illegal. Just please leave me alone and let me do this on my own."

"Oh, Maddy," said her mother. "Maddy, we love you."

"I know," Maddy whispered.

Her father cleared his throat. "Well, can we see it when it's done?" he asked.

Maddy hesitated. "I don't know," she said.

"You don't know?" asked her mother. "But you've always shown us your artwork. We're so proud of you. We've always supported—"

"It's just something I have to do," Maddy repeated, lowering her hands. "It's hard. I don't know where it's going. All I know is it's helping."

"It *is* helping?" asked her father, his voice quiet but steady. "You're sure? You promise us that?"

"Yes," said Maddy, her eyes downcast, but her voice going out to meet her father's. "Yes, I promise."

The tension relaxed somewhat. "Maddy, sweetie," whispered her mother. "We just want you back."

"I'm here," said Maddy. "I'm still me."

A look passed between her parents. Maddy didn't see it but she felt it – encyclopedic with all they weren't saying. Again, her father cleared his throat.

"So you want to work on this project on your own, without any of us looking at it?" he asked.

"Yes," said Maddy.

"On one condition," said her father.

Maddy's heart clenched.

"Look at me, Maddikins," said her father.

With a deep breath, Maddy forced her eyes up to meet his.

"Promise you'll tell us if it gets to be too much?" he asked.

The fear clenching Maddy's heart let go. Breath came back. "Yes," she said quickly. "I promise."

Her father's eyes held onto her face, searching. "Okay, then," he said. "That's enough for me. Delores?"

Delores Malone sighed. "Yes," she said. "Yes, okay."

"Leanne?" asked Mr. Malone.

Leanne blew out a mini-cyclone of air. "I guess," she muttered.

For a moment no one spoke, the silence this time gentle, patting things back into place. "I'm about to start the crossword puzzle," said Mr. Malone. "Lend me your brain, Leanne?"

"Sure," said Leanne, and they headed into the living room. Side by side, Maddy and her mother returned to Monday supper prep.

"You *will* tell us, Maddy," her mother said, her voice sing-songy with anxiety. "For sure?"

Maddy leaned her forehead against the cupboard door and let its coolness enter her flushed face. She thought of Nikki, and everything Nikki probably hadn't told her parents.

"Yes," she said steadily. "When I can, I'll tell you everything."

• • •

Tuesday afternoon Ms. Mousumi was back, though still sniffling. As Maddy sank into her seat, Lilian Pickersgill got up from her desk near the center of the first row and approached the teacher's desk. Over the class chatter, Maddy heard Lilian explain that she was next in line to read a chapter of *The Pain*

Eater. Ms. Mousumi thanked her for the information and Lilian returned to her seat. Lilian was a top student, the kind who read ahead in textbooks out of curiosity. Silently, Maddy heaped blessings upon the other girl's head.

It was the last day for group work, and they were finishing up a series of questions regarding Jeannette Armstrong's short story "Blue Against White." Vince and August sat down with characteristic abandon; David slid carefully into place. Without hesitation, August took over, leading the discussion. Vince and David chipped in the odd response; Maddy sat digging her right thumbnail into her left hand. It still helped; it still gave her something to focus on that kept the internal craziness at bay. Directly in front of her, grinning up from her binder cover, was the mask decal. Maddy's gaze lifted from her hands to the decal. Then it flicked across to David, who was busy writing something down. She glanced back at her hands. The thing was, she realized, today she wasn't feeling the usual craziness for some reason, the sick swell of fear that told her the memories were close, they were about to take shape. Today, she didn't feel caught between two worlds, the inner and the outer. No, today, she felt as if she was in one place – this classroom – and it was okay. She was here, sitting three feet away from David Janklow, whom she was now certain had never had any intention of hurting her, and she was managing.

Her right thumbnail lifted out of the welt it had just imprinted in her left hand. As if it had a mind of its own, its own tiny, separate brain, it rose from her lap and settled onto the cover of her binder, where it began to wedge itself under the edge of the mask decal. To her surprise, the decal lifted easily, peeling off the plastic surface in one piece. Without hesitation, she crumpled it into a tiny wad.

When she looked up, David was watching her. His gaze was riveted, as if he were observing something cataclysmic, like the birth of Frankenstein. Maddy's voice came out cool and even, as if it had been waiting for this moment, as if it had been intending it. "Do you want this?" she asked, holding the wad out to him. David shook his head. Getting to her feet, Maddy walked to the garbage pail beside Ms. Mousumi's desk and deposited the crumpled decal. Then she returned to her seat.

"You got anything to say about this story?" August asked her, one eyebrow raised.

"Not really," said Maddy, her gaze flicking away.

With a sigh, August moved on, poking and prodding con-tributions out of Vince and David. Unrepentant, Maddy sat staring at her binder cover. It was gone. The leering, sneering reminder of her fear and humiliation had been destroyed. And it had been destroyed by *her*. She breathed in slowly, feeling the air travel in through her nose and deep into her lungs, as if some kind of invisible barrier had been removed.

Maddy smiled slightly; it was her own smile – not a mask.

• • •

Lilian Pickersgill rose from her seat and walked to the front of the class. Chubby, with glasses, she was involved in everything from the Science Club to Student Council. Hers was the kind of mind that operated like an origami project, taking what seemed to be flat and nondescript and folding it into the unexpected. As she halted beside Ms. Mousumi's desk and turned on her tablet, the class straightened in their desks.

"The high priestess sat in her office, playing with the soul stones," began Lilian. "A crescent moon was in the sky. The high priestess was doing her usual hexing, but she was bored. Things were going okay in the tribe. Everyone was afraid of her, even Farang. Everyone was obeying her and toeing the line. Like Emeka said, Farang had to die sometime soon, but not quite yet. Still, the high priestess needed to stir things up. She was just that kind of gal.

"She picked up Farang's soul stone and held it to her forehead. She closed her eyes and concentrated. She thought of every bit of Farang's face and body – the way she moved and talked. Then the high priestess shapeshifted into an exact double of Farang, even down to her clothes, which were tattered.

"Once she thought she looked exactly like Farang, the high priestess went to a bronze mirror to check herself out. *Perfect!* she thought, staring at herself. No one, not even Farang, could tell the difference between them. So she had to be careful, but not too careful. Everyone except her was asleep, or was supposed to be. So she could get away with everything she planned to do.

"The high priestess crept out of the temple and into the village. Then she snuck in and out of people's huts, wrecking and stealing things. Each time, after she was finished, she stood over the bed of someone sleeping in the hut and sort of woke them up. Not all the way – just partway, so they saw her looking down at them but were so sleepy they fell right back to sleep. In the morning, when they woke and found things broken and stolen, they remembered Farang and got mad at her.

"Of course, the villagers weren't allowed to talk to Farang. So they couldn't ask her why she was in their huts, or about the wrecked stuff. But they could yell and throw things at her. They could follow her around, and even kick and hit her. Which is what they did. Things got really ugly for Farang. She wasn't safe anywhere, except deep in the forest all alone. The temple priestesses fed her every day, but she couldn't get near that food anymore, because that was where the villagers waited to get at her. So she began to get very thin and weak.

"The high priestess watched all this with glee. It made her evil heart rejoice. She did this every night for over a week – she shapeshifted into Farang and wrecked the village. The villagers started to post guards, but still the high priestess got past them because she could shapeshift into a bug and crawl past them in the dark. Then she shapeshifted to Farang inside a hut, and did the usual.

"Farang had no idea what the high priestess was doing. She was just always running for her life.

"Then one night, the high priestess shapeshifted into Farang again. She got into the chief's hut, and into the jewelry of his wives. In Faraway, there was a special stone they called the 'kulumulu.' It was like a diamond – clear and glittering, but it could change colors, almost as if it was alive. If it changed color while you held it in your hand, it had you in its power until it changed color again. And that's what happened to the high priestess. She touched one of the chief's kulumulus, and it changed color – from yellow to azure. And what this did – it trapped the high priestess into Farang's shape. The high priestess knew as soon as it happened, and she knew she was in big trouble.

"She knew her only chance was to keep the kulumulu and try to get it to shapeshift her back. She could still hex and throw spells, so she cast a sleeping spell on the guy guarding the hut and got past him. But after that, she couldn't go back to the temple. None of the other priestesses had ever seen her shapeshift *at all*. So they'd never believe her if she told them she wasn't Farang, she was the high priestess. No, she had to hide out in the forest just like Farang, until she could get the kulumulu to change color again. Or who knows – when it came to Farang's time to die, the tribe might kill the high priestess by mistake. That's what you get for playing with fire. Or other people's souls."

With an impish grin, Lilian shut off her tablet. "That's it," she said, turning to Ms. Mousumi. Ms. Mousumi gave her an impish grin back.

"Interesting plot twist," said the teacher. "You've certainly set things up for our next writer, who is...let me see."

She reached for her class list, but two seats over from Maddy, Theresa Pronk raised her hand. "I'm next," she said. "I had something planned, but this totally screws it up."

Lilian arched a pleased eyebrow and headed for her seat. Impressed, the class watched her sit down. "Any comments?" asked Ms. Mousumi.

Silence replied. The class was in deep thought. Then Paul's hand went up.

"Can *we* kill her off?" he asked, his face intense. The class erupted into laughter. Paul flushed sheepishly.

"The high priestess or Farang?" asked Harvir, grinning at him.

"The high priestess!" replied Paul, looking shocked.

Harvir nodded without speaking. Glancing at Dana, Julie grimaced.

"That will be up to Theresa," said Ms. Mousumi. She consulted her attendance sheet. "Or, after Thanksgiving – Amy Rupp and Ken Soong."

At the mention of Ken's name, Maddy jerked, and her eyes darted to Ken, who was sitting leaned back, his gaze on Ms. Mousumi. Beside him, David continued to sit visibly tilted away. Returning to her desk, Maddy's eyes settled onto her binder, its clean green surface. The mask decal had been gone for one day. So far, there had been no response from Ken, so it appeared David hadn't told him. Gently, tentatively, Maddy's hand crept across the binder cover. Green had always been her favorite color – she used to see it and happiness would open wide within her. If happiness wasn't opening wide now, still she could feel a glimmer of it – a memory of how she used to feel, and the hope she would someday feel that way again. It was the beginning of something new, or of something known and beloved coming back to her. Either way, she wasn't going to let go of it. For the life of her, no goddamn mask decal was getting anywhere near her person or her belongings again. When

Maddy glanced at Ken this time, she felt angry. With a deep breath, she placed both palms flat on her binder. The back of her left hand was completely free of thumbnail welts.

• • •

The tree house mural was taking discernible form. Seven trees now rose out of the turbulent, shifting ground, their branches startled, even terrified-looking. Earlier that afternoon, Maddy had altered her usual route home from school and walked past the actual copse, where she'd counted the aspens. There were sixteen. In the October afternoon light, they had loomed over her, wind-stripped, the odd remaining leaf rustling a warning in the breeze. She'd felt jumpy, standing alone there – her heart thudding painfully – but she'd held herself in place like a live grasshopper in a closed hand, and made herself look around. There, between those two trees – that was where they'd pushed her down. She could see the tree root that had wedged itself into the middle of her back, and the open area between two other trees to which David had retreated. Until he'd read his chapter of *The Pain Eater*, she'd assumed he was standing lookout. Now, it seemed, he'd been shocked, afraid, and simply hadn't known what to do – then or now.

Neither did Maddy. Other than what she was doing here in the tree house, that is. To her right stood a kerosene lamp her father had given her to use, now that the evenings had grown dark. To either side of it, she'd propped a large flashlight. Sixteen trees, she decided, were too many. Seven would have to do. Getting to her feet, she started to sketch in the glow of a streetlight, the one that had hovered over David's head as he'd stood at the edge of the copse. It was smaller than the first cream-gold sphere that she'd drawn high up on the wall, above the trees and the half moon that now sat caught in an aspen's branches. Maddy could not have said what that original glowing sphere was; she knew only that it had been part of the mural's beginning, and everything that followed was connected to it. Compared to that sphere, the streetlights were dim and useless – they began and ended nothing. They hadn't saved, or even helped, her.

But they had been there. And Maddy wanted to record everything that had been present, down to the last, terrifying detail – to know all of it, to be able to point to it and say, *Here*. And, *This*. And then, *This here*.

Sometimes, as she drew, her heart knuckle-punched and kicked. The mural felt like a bruise under her hand, the chalk like sticks of pain. But it was pain leaving her, flowing out of herself and onto the wall.

She shifted position, and began to work on another streetlight.

chapter thirteen

Theresa Pronk was a tall, plump girl who'd had several poems published in the student newspaper. She played flute in the school band, and had helped Maddy paint sets for last spring's production of *Our Town*. Deceptively docile-looking, she fit well into any background, where she muttered nonstop comments that kept anyone nearby in stitches. As she made her way to the front of Friday's class, Maddy watched with interest.

"It was hunger that did it," Theresa began. "Farang's name meant 'hunger,' and now she couldn't get the food she needed from the temple because the villagers kept attacking her. It was summer, so cold wasn't a problem, but still she grew weak and ill. She stopped going into the village, and ate roots and berries, and hung out at her secret altar. As she grew weaker, she crossed over in her mind. She started to have visions of The Beautiful Land without needing to eat the allura poison.

"Like Julie said, in The Beautiful Land, Farang was beautiful. She was loved and had family and friends. It was a far, far better place than here on earth for her. And now that she could get there on her own, she went there and stayed there. Day after day, she lay by her secret altar with her eyes closed, and wandered around The Beautiful Land inside her head. She got thinner and thinner. She felt as if she was breathing life out, instead of breathing it in. Farang was dying and she knew it, but she didn't care. She didn't care about anything anymore.

"Meanwhile, the high priestess was still sneaking around, looking exactly like Farang. She had the kulumulu stone in a leather pouch around her neck, waiting for it to change color so she could go back to being herself again. She also had to keep out of the village so she wouldn't be attacked, and she had to live on roots and berries like Farang. So she got thin and weak, too. Then one day she walked deeper into the forest than usual, and saw Farang lying by her altar and dreaming about The Beautiful Land.

"The high priestess's first thought was to take a stone from the altar and bash in Farang's head. But Farang was the pain eater. Lousy as that job was, it was protected by the gods. If the high priestess killed Farang, the gods would take vengeance on *her*. So she decided on a different plan.

"She knelt over Farang and shook her so she opened her eyes. When Farang saw her exact twin, she screamed. The high priestess put a hand over Farang's mouth until she calmed down. Then she said, 'I am your soul. You wanted to get me back, and now I've come back to you. You're in great danger, and I know how to save you. But you must do exactly as I say.'

"Farang nodded. She believed the high priestess completely. After all, nothing like this had ever happened to her before. Sure, she'd seen the high priestess shapeshift into a tiger, but she never suspected anything like *this*. So she did what the high priestess ordered. She hunted for nuts and berries for them both, and gave the best to the high priestess to eat. She built a lean-to for them to sleep under, and stole a blanket from a hut to cover them at night. The high priestess didn't help any – she just sat around, staring at the kulumulu stone and muttering. But Farang didn't worry about that at first, because she was so happy to have her soul back. After a while, though, it started to bug her. Her soul just sat there, eating and complaining. A couple of times, she even slapped Farang. What kind of loser soul was that? Farang started to wish her soul had never come back to her.

"But the high priestess was working on a plan. At the night of the full moon, she followed Farang to the village and hid nearby. One of the three priestesses who was left did the ceremony – everyone thought a tiger had gotten the high priestess. Then, when Farang started crawling out of the bushes, the high priestess came out too – but walking.

"The villagers were amazed. In ancient times, twins were thought to be a miracle. The high priestess knew this, and it was part of her plan. The villagers fell on their faces before her, and the high priestess held up a hand and called, 'Be silent! The gods are here to speak to you!'

"Farang was pretty surprised. It was news to her that her

soul was a god. But so far, so good. So she just stood up and watched her soul talk to the villagers.

"'The gods have decided to reward you,' said the high priestess. 'They've sent you a sign. I am that sign. The gods know you've been suffering. They know you've had to feel extra pain because your pain eater disobeyed. Your pain eater refused to accept her destiny. Instead, she's stealing and wrecking things. Now you're angry and want to kill her. That's why I've come – to remind you of the *good* purpose of the pain eater. Remember, the pain eater's destiny is from the gods. The pain eater dies when the *gods* decide it. Until then, the pain eater has to eat your pain. She eats your pain, and I rule over you for the gods and keep you all safe.'

"No one dared challenge the high priestess – they were too much in awe of her as Farang's twin. They just believed her. So she took over the ceremony, and commanded the people to dance as Farang crawled into the cage. She even had some allura leaf powder in a pouch, and she secretly sprinkled it onto Farang's food before she put it into the cage. So everything went as it usually did, with Farang twisting and screaming, and floating off to The Beautiful Land in her head.

"But when Farang came back, she was changed. She was angry. If this was the way souls behaved, then Farang decided she didn't need one. As far as she was concerned, her soul was fired. But the other villagers were impressed with Farang's soul – they truly believed she was a sign from the gods. But Farang knew something fishy was going on. Still, she knew there was one thing her soul said that was true – she *was* in great danger.

There were now two of her running around: a good twin and an evil twin. Farang was the good twin and her soul was evil. But all the villagers thought it was the other way around. It was kind of like living in a mirror – a mirror you never wanted to look at. A mirror you wanted to smash, so it would all go away."

Theresa lowered the pages she was reading from, and gave the class an uncertain smile. "Over to you, Amy," she said to the girl sitting beside Jeremy. Amy's shoulders slumped.

"Okay, Theresa," said Ms. Mousumi, getting to her feet. "Thank you. Any comments?"

As Theresa headed for her seat, a number of hands went up. "I like that twins are a gift from the gods," said Brent Doody with a broad grin. "I'll have to tell Bobby."

The class burst into laughter. Brent and Bob Doody, fraternal twins, were both high profile in the cafeteria video games crowd.

"I think it's only identical twins," said Theresa, bopping him on the head with her rolled-up pages as she sat down behind him. "No luck, Doody."

Brent collapsed in apparent desolation. "Yes, Jeremy?" said Ms. Mousumi.

"What I don't get," said Jeremy, one desk in front of Maddy, "is why Farang never gets ahead. No matter what happens to her in this story, she always ends up exactly where she started."

"That's an interesting point," said the teacher.

"Yeah," Harvir threw in from across the room. "It's almost like *we* believe in her destiny. We live now, in modern times, but we still think like they did. It's weird," he added, his voice trailing off.

"What does everyone else think?" asked Ms. Mousumi. "This is an interesting point that's been raised here. Has our thinking on destiny changed since ancient times? Do we all still believe in it?"

The class sat musing. Julie raised her hand.

"It depends on who you are," she said. "If you're born poor, and your family is starving in a third world country, you're probably going to stay poor. But if you're born middle class or rich over here…." She shrugged.

"How about at this school?" asked Ms. Mousumi. "How does our thinking on destiny affect the way we treat each other here?"

Eyebrows rose as students considered the question. Nikki's hand went up.

"Your rep's everything," she said. "Once you've got one, consider it your destiny until kingdom come."

"It can't be changed?" asked Ms. Mousumi.

"A *good* rep can change," said Nikki, "but once you're down, you can't come back up."

A knowing smile appeared on the face of Sean Longstreet, who sat to Nikki's left. Letting her gaze slide past him, Maddy saw the same smile appear on the faces of a sequence of guys, sitting side by side – Sean, Elliot, Harvir, Ken, and David. No, not David. In contrast to the others, he was looking downward, his expression uncomfortable. But to his right, Julie, Dana, and Christine wore similar smiles. Smirks.

Ms. Mousumi obviously didn't want to delve deeply into the topic of fallen reputations. "Okay, class, we'll leave it there," she said. "Today, we're working on…"

Maddy's gaze left the teacher and settled on Rhonda Hinkle, who sat opposite her in the front row. Rhonda, she realized suddenly – the only obviously disabled student – was also the only one who'd gone directly against the rest of the students' penchant for destiny. Stalwart in her oddly leaning body, she'd faced down the class and proclaimed, "I can!" Rhonda wasn't a popular student. Rarely did someone join her as she made her determined swaying way through the halls. In situations where a class had to divide into smaller groups of choice, she was usually left standing alone. To her shame, Maddy couldn't recall ever having spoken to Rhonda.

Her gaze drifted sideways, to Kara's still-empty seat. *No*, she realized. Rhonda wasn't the only one who'd refused to surrender Farang to a destiny determined by others. Kara had gotten the whole plot going by stating that Farang stopped believing in her destiny at age fifteen. How was Kara doing? Maddy wondered. Had her brother's funeral taken place yet? What did *she* think now about destiny – after Frank's suicide?

More than anything, she wished suddenly, deeply, that Kara was back among them – with her sarcastic, savvy comments, the bitter bite of her knowing. Kara wouldn't have let Nikki's comment about fallen reputations stand. She wouldn't have put up with the class's repeated return to the status quo, in *The Pain Eater* or in real life. For the first time since the assault in March, Maddy felt the flicker of the desire to talk to someone in particular, to a friend.

• • •

Two blocks from school, they were on her. Maddy was crossing a strip-mall parking lot on her way home, when a group of guys on bikes sped past. "Hey!" one of them hollered. "Get a load of this – it's Maddy Malone!"

Like a flock of birds, they turned en masse and came back toward her. Startled, not quite getting it yet, Maddy edged to one side to give them room, but they swooped in closer and began to circle her. All were familiar as hallway faces; she knew two first names. There were six in total.

"Oooo, Maddy!" sang one. "We've heard about *you*, Maddy."

"Maddy Malone," called another. "Maddy's mad for it – she's *mad* for it."

On all sides, bikes whirred and clanged. Maddy couldn't take a step in any direction without smashing into spinning metal, a leering, sneering face. Beyond the hooting circle, cars dotted the parking lot; traffic continued to stream past on an adjoining commuter road; a few people went into a nearby bank. No one gave a second glance at what was going on, what was happening to Maddy right before their eyes.

"Ooo Maddy, we *know* about you," jeered a voice.

A sick feeling oozed through Maddy's gut. With it came the memory of other voices, of panting and grunting. Darkness swelled inside her mind; a streetlight came on, faint in the distance. Raising both arms, Maddy wrapped them over her head.

"An egg," crowed someone. "You're an egg, Maddy – over easy, over easy."

Then, just as quickly as they'd appeared, they were gone, the whir of their bikes fading. Still, it was a while before Maddy lowered her arms. The voices and shapes in her mind were too intense; imaginary hands continued to grab at her and push her down, and she couldn't break free of them, couldn't get up, *couldn't get up.*

And then she could. Like the parting of a dense fog, the dark, grunting shapes in her mind dissolved. Maddy opened her eyes to see an elderly woman peering at her, a look of concern on her face.

"Are you all right, dear?" she asked. "Would you like me to call someone?"

Maddy stood blinking at her. After the mess inside her head, this ordinary woman's face felt like an alternate reality, an image on an electronic billboard. Without speaking, she turned from the woman and headed across the parking lot. Home – all she could think of was home and the tree house, where she could be alone without anyone coming at her on bikes, riding their own loaded jeers. *Mad Maddy. Over easy, over easy.* Maddy's face burned. She'd never heard a girl being taunted with the latter phrase, but there was only one possible meaning to attach to it. Which meant that someone had talked. After seven months, finally, one of the five had told. Not David – somehow Maddy was certain of this – but Ken or Pete, Robbie, or the fifth, as-yet-unidentified participant. Whoever it was, if these bike thugs knew, everyone at school soon would. The comments coming her way then would leave "Over easy" in the dust.

Maddy's gut exploded like a mushroom cloud. Bending over, she vomited onto the sidewalk.

• • •

Thanksgiving weekend passed in a blur. Leaving the city on Saturday morning, the Malones drove for several hours to Middle Lake, where Ian Malone's parents still farmed. A two-day romp of cousins and tail-wagging collies – Maddy tried not to freak at all the noise, the continual pressure of love and friendliness she was expected to return. On her left inner thigh, a new burn blister festered. She'd tried to resist the urge, to hold off, but had surrendered late Friday evening. Now, even under a bandage, it stung and rubbed against her jeans. She'd held the cigarette ember too long against her leg – she'd known it at the time – but the numbness it brought had felt so good, just peace and quiet in her head....

"Is she eating enough?" she overheard her grandmother ask her mother. "She's so pale. Maybe she's anemic."

All weekend, Maddy made an effort to eat extra and to compliment her grandmother on her cooking. It was hard, forcing herself to keep at it. She felt so tired, as if a great weight pushed down on her. Gears ground continually in her head, and a slow fog seemed to have settled in around her. All she wanted was to give in and float off into nothingness, but her grandmother watched so closely, and her grandfather kept asking her to go out for a stroll. For two days, Maddy strolled and stuffed herself. Finally, Monday arrived, and she was once again in the family car and homeward bound. Beside her, Leanne sat texting nonstop on her phone; in the front, Gordon Lightfoot warbled from the dash as her parents discussed her mother's new work schedule. Staring out a side window, Maddy let her mind go into a deadman's float. In a deadman's float, nothing came into her head. And nothing was fine with her – nothing about the past, nothing about what was coming. *Nothing, nothing, nothing – everything was nothing,* she *was nothing....*

The car pulled into the front drive. Doors opened, bodies piled out and began pulling at overnight bags. Knapsack over a shoulder, a sleeping bag under one arm, Maddy followed her father to the front door. There he paused, digging in his pocket for his keys. "What's this?" he asked, reaching for something white that hung from the doorknob.

It was a mask – a cheap plastic Greek comedy mask – an exact replica of the ones handed out at *Our Town.* Lifting it off the doorknob by its elastic head string, Ian Malone examined it. "Huh," he said. "Some kind of advertising? There's no logo on it." With a shrug, he unlocked the door, walked into the front vestibule, and hung the mask on a coat tree. The next few minutes were filled with coming and going as the car was unpacked and family belongings trekked into the house. By the time the last car door slammed and the front vestibule had been cleared out, the Greek comedy mask had disappeared from the coat tree – with no one but Maddy to see as she crushed it repeatedly underfoot into the driveway asphalt then kicked the fragments into the brisk fall wind.

chapter fourteen

Maddy sat, hunched in her desk. Around her, the English classroom buzzed with chatter, complemented by frequent bursts of laughter. Each fresh burst came at Maddy like an attack of sound, like a wave of electric shock. Already, multiple thumbnail welts rode the back of her left hand. From across the room, by the entrance, she could feel it – Ken's dark stare glommed onto her. Assessing…she was sure of it. Ken was watching her and assessing the effects of The Masked Avengers' master plan put into action.

All day, she'd been getting comments. Not every minute and not from everyone, but there were guys grinning at her in the halls who'd never noticed her before, and girls with knowing smirks. She didn't know half their names, but all of them now seemed to know hers. Nobody said anything *exactly*. It was all vague references about wanting *it*, being mad for *it*. No one mentioned last March, *Our Town*, or a copse of aspen…four guys jumping her under the cover of evening darkness, while one stood by. Nothing about *that*.

When she'd checked her Twitter at lunch, there had been mentions from unfamiliar accounts. The usernames didn't identify the senders by their real names; Maddy had no idea if they were The Masked Avengers in a new disguise or someone to whom The Masked Avengers had passed her username. These tweets had been like the hallway comments she'd been getting, but more specific: *Blow me, blow me, blow me, baby*. And *I hear Malone's a busy place these days. Can I check in?* And *You lookin' to learn the splitz? I can teach ya.* Maddy had blocked all three accounts. Then she'd gone to the nearest girls' washroom and thrown up in a toilet.

About her now, the class went quiet. As if someone had flicked a switch, every mouth simultaneously stopped talking. Cued by the abrupt silence, Maddy glanced up to see Kara Adovasio hesitating by the classroom entrance. Half the kids in the room were staring at her, the rest gazing pointedly elsewhere. Kara herself looked stunned, as if she'd been caught in the glare of headlights. Ducking her head, she strode across the front of the room. Ms. Mousumi greeted her as she passed the teacher's desk, and then Kara was slipping around behind Maddy and into her empty seat.

Maddy didn't know what to do. One row ahead, Jeremy sat, his back rigid as he stared directly ahead. No one turned to Kara and smiled, welcoming her back. Without a word, Kara took out her phone and began thumbing. She looked pale, her chestnut hair pulled into a careless ponytail. The expression on her face warned everyone off. The old Kara was back, multiplied ten times over.

Inexplicably, Maddy found herself wondering what Kara's stomach felt like. She wondered if the inside of the other girl's thighs were clear, or festering, like her own, with cigarette burns. Were gears grinding in her head – was she looking constantly for a way to turn them off, to sink into the relief of clear, still nothingness?

Opening her binder, Maddy tore out a piece of foolscap. In neat square letters, she wrote, *I'm very very sorry about your brother. I hope you'll be okay.* Then she folded it and passed it to Kara.

Kara's eyes darted to the extended note, and she stared at it a moment before taking it. Then she opened and read it. Her mouth sucked in, and Maddy watched her fight off the urge to cry. Tearing off a blank section from Maddy's note, Kara wrote something and passed it back to Maddy. The actual note, she tucked into a shirt pocket.

Maddy read the note. *Thank you*, it said. *Everywhere I go, nobody says anything. They stare like I'm the end of the world, but they don't say anything.* That was it – nothing further. Kara didn't look at her, didn't reach out and touch the back of Maddy's hand and say, *Stop doing that.* But Maddy stopped. Letting both hands lie still, she allowed herself to fill with the meaning of the note: She, Maddy Malone, had done something no one else had done. She'd shown courage where others had shown only fear. It was a small thing, maybe, but it had changed the world slightly for Kara. And it had changed the world for Maddy. Somewhere inside herself, the empty hole punched open by that day's smirks and tweets began to close over. Maddy no longer felt as if she was pouring out of herself like a lost river. Carefully, she slid Kara's reply note into her binder's front inside pocket.

• • •

Maddy sat on her heels, observing the tree house mural. Seven trees now arched their frightened branches, and several streetlights glowed in the distance. There were no stars, but then she hadn't drawn a horizon line – the swirling ground simply rose up and became a muttering sky. Focusing on that swirling ground-sky, Maddy tried to let it talk to her. Shifts of black and gray, groans of brown – it was as if she'd taken the inside of her gut and placed it on the tree house wall. If she reached out and touched the dark mural, she would be touching herself – her pain, her heartbeat. Her terror, and the shape of that terror. For so long, Maddy hadn't wanted to give form to her fear; all she'd wanted was for it to go away, to vanish. Now, she was calling that night back to herself; her hands ached to touch the memory bit by bit, as much as she could handle.

Her palms were actually throbbing. *There*, she thought, fixing on a spot between the trees. *Right there.* Rising to her knees, she touched a stick of chalk to the wall, and began to draw the first figure.

• • •

English class emitted the usual dull roar. As Maddy entered the classroom and turned right, she heard her name called, but didn't bother to look. Several times earlier that day, guys had spoken to her in the halls; smirks and snickers had followed her everywhere. Or that was the way it felt. At her locker, before homeroom, she'd gotten several comments; after that, like a house of mirrors, every face seemed to reflect the same taunts and sneers.

In addition, her Twitter was growing popular; before breakfast, she'd blocked several new followers, and nine at lunch. Her notifications had also skyrocketed. Previously, on a good day, she might have registered five mentions; her current number stood at nineteen. After reading the first few, Maddy had closed the app. It wasn't a conscious decision – her mind had gone numb and shut down, and her hand had taken over, doing the thinking for her: *No more. No more.*

Maddy simply didn't know how to respond to what was coming at her, what to do with any of it. Like yesterday, the tweets and comments slipslid definition; they referred to nothing in particular and at the same time insinuated everything. How did one fight back against innuendo? How was she supposed to take on a rumor without knowing what that rumor claimed? Sitting down at her desk, she took out her phone and began thumbing. Beside her, Kara was occupied likewise. Since their note-passing episode yesterday, they hadn't spoken, and at the moment Maddy didn't feel up to it.

A paper airplane sailed between their desks and crashed into the wall behind them. Without hesitating, Kara swivelled in her seat and picked up the crumpled missive, then unfolded it and read the message scrawled inside. Her mouth dropped open in disbelief.

"Who sent this?" she asked Maddy.

"I dunno," Maddy replied. Unwillingly, but unable to resist, she read the note Kara held out for her to read: *Party time, bitch. A baker's dozen – twelve guys and you. Don't you like those odds?*

Shock slammed Maddy, followed by something heated and ugly. *Shame.* Face on fire, she ducked her head.

"What the fuck is this supposed to mean?" demanded Kara. "I want to know who wrote it." With a hiss, she crumpled the note, just as Ms. Mousumi got to her feet and called Amy Rupp to the front of the room. Looking nervous, Amy rose from her seat beside Jeremy. Nondescript, she tended to fit into the background like Theresa, but without the humorous asides. Nothing about her stood out; she took up an average amount of space and went along to get along. When she reached the front of the class, Amy took a moment to scan her first paragraph. Then she glanced up. Briefly, her gaze locked with Julie's.

"Farang knew she was beaten," Amy began. "There was no way she was ever going to change things. At least not for herself. But there was one thing she could do. She could get even.

"Farang decided to become her evil twin. She decided to *become* her evil rep. Everyone already thought that was the way she was, and it'd be a lot more fun than the way she was living now.

"She snuck into huts at night and stole things. Mostly she

stole things to eat – her name was 'Hunger,' wasn't it? But she also stole jewels and clothes, and stuff like that. One night, she stole a kulumulu necklace. She didn't know what it could do, she just liked it. An hour later, the kulumulu necklace changed color. When it did, Farang was thinking about the high priestess – how much she hated her and wanted to kill her. So the kulumulu necklace made Farang shapeshift into the high priestess.

"Farang didn't know until she went to the river to take a bath. When she looked in the water, she saw the high priestess, and that's when she got it – that she now looked exactly like her. She also figured out that her 'soul' was the real high priestess. So Farang made up a story to tell the tribe. She said that she was gone for a while because she was kidnapped by bandits. But then she escaped and came back. Farang told this lie to the village and the priestesses. Everyone believed her. Because the high priestess *was* missing for a while, so this looked like a true reason.

"The real high priestess was still at the temple, pretending to be Farang's soul. Farang knew this wasn't true, of course. Just like the high priestess knew who the fake high priestess really was. So there you had it – the high priestess and Farang both looked like each other, and they both hated each other. Both of them wanted to kill each other too, and they plotted in secret. Then the next full moon came around. Of course, no one could find the real Farang to eat the pain. So Farang, looking like the high priestess, said Farang's soul had to do the job. So there was the high priestess, looking like Farang, crawling out of the bushes and getting spat on by the villagers. Then the real Farang, looking like the high priestess, leaned over her to spit her pain onto her too. But at that moment, both kulumulu stones changed color again. So Farang and the high priestess *both* shapeshifted back to themselves. So *then* the real Farang ended up in the cage, and the real high priestess was back in the temple. Y'see, a leopard can't change its spots. It might be able to hide them for a while, but they always come back. The end."

A hand went up. "You forgot something," said Theresa. "There was no allura leaf poison in the food this time."

Amy blushed, as if guilty of something. "Why not?" she asked.

"Only the high priestess knew about it," said Theresa. "She was the one putting it into the food for Farang. But this time, she was the one *getting* the food, so she couldn't have put it in."

Another hand went up. "Maybe she put it in at the last minute," said Julie. "*After* she shapeshifted."

"How would she have any?" asked Theresa. "She was Farang's soul up to the last second before they both shapeshifted back, and she didn't know *that* was going to happen. So she wouldn't have been ready for it. That means the real Farang crawled into the cage and ate food without poison for the first time. So she didn't feel any pain. She's gotta wonder about that."

"Yeah," burst out Paul. "Maybe *that's* why she stops believing when she's fifteen. She figures out the high priestess usually poisons the food and *that's* why she feels pain – *not* because the villagers are giving her their pain."

Ms. Mousumi got to her feet. "Okay, Amy – you can sit down now. I'm wondering what Kara thinks of all this. Have you had a chance to catch up on the chapters you missed, Kara?"

"Yeah," said Kara. "I followed them on the website." She shrugged, her face expressionless. "I guess it's like any assignment – some kids follow the instructions, and some don't. But so what? It's not my story – only the first chapter was."

Ms. Mousumi hesitated, as if discomfited by Kara's uncharacteristic lack of interest. The entire class, in fact, looked openly surprised, a few even disappointed. Something had obviously changed for Kara, big time. *I guess*, thought Maddy, darting a sideways glance at the other girl, *if your brother died, you wouldn't care much about a story anymore. About anything, really.*

"Well," said Ms. Mousumi. "We'll have to leave that to Ken Soong to solve. So, Ken – Friday? And after Ken, we have two more to go – Sheng Yoo and August Zire. Okay, class, open your books to…"

Tuning out of the teacher's instructions, Maddy pulled a piece of foolscap from her binder. Across it, she wrote: *What do you really think about* The Pain Eater *– how it's going?* She passed it to Kara.

Kara considered before responding. *I think most of it's crap,* she wrote back under Maddy's original note. *But that's like the rest of life – most people don't want to really think. It's no different here.*

Maddy read and reread Kara's reply. She hesitated. Her heart pounded. Then she wrote: *How are you? Are you suffering a lot?* She passed the note to Kara.

Kara stared at Maddy's latest words. She blinked quickly;

her mouth twisted in, then relaxed into a weak smile. Turning to Maddy, she looked directly at her.

"Thanks for asking," she whispered. Then she turned her attention back to Ms. Mousumi. Maddy took a moment longer to tune in to the teacher's words. She was shifting around inside herself, trying to get used to the feeling that had just come over her. The sensation wasn't new, but it had been a long time since she'd experienced it. It was the feeling of connection – the feeling of belonging in the world of the living. She was no longer a bump on a log, a thing that had been destroyed by fear. Not that she was no longer afraid – some of the recent comments and tweets she'd received had sent fear roaring through her. But somewhere inside herself, over the past six weeks, she'd grown strong enough so that she was now ready to take on that fear. It was no longer so big that it shut her down completely. Which meant there was room inside for something besides terror. For the first time, Maddy found herself wondering what *she* had to say about *The Pain Eater*. Not that it mattered – Ken had manipulated her out of the sequence of readers, and it looked like her chance was a goner – but what would she say *if* she got that chance back?

Whatever that might be, first she was going to have to listen to Ken's contribution.

• • •

It was the following day. Afternoon classes had ended, and Maddy was on her way out of the school. To her right, the art room door stood open. Inside, she could hear chattering, followed by a wave of boisterous laughter. Maddy's footsteps slowed; she paused to listen. From the outside, the art room always sounded like so much fun. *If*, she reminded herself, *you aren't Jenn, or someone else Mr. Zarro takes a dislike to. Still*, she thought wistfully, *I'm not Jenn. Do I have to suffer for her for the rest of high school?* Maddy missed art class, the chance to open up to possibilities of color and form. And Jenn didn't even know what Maddy had foregone for her sake. *What does it matter in the end?* Maddy wondered. Was she helping Jenn by not taking art? What was the point?

"Hey!" said a voice. "It's Malone."

Before Maddy could respond, three guys had surrounded her. One of them she knew by name – Rory McBriar, a guy from her math class. The rest were hallway faces.

"Oooo hooo!" sang Rory. "Mad Maddy. Watcha doin', Maddy?" He edged in, crowding her, and Maddy backed up to give herself space. Rory moved in again.

"Maddy, Maddy," cooed another guy, "come over to my house to play. Oooo – come over to my house to *fuck*, Mad Maddy."

They were crowding in closer now, all three to her left. Again, Maddy moved right to give herself room. "Back off!" she said, raising her left arm. Rory grabbed it, just as a door opened to Maddy's right and a guy emerged, releasing the sound of flushing toilets.

"Quick!" said Rory, and all three grabbed Maddy and pushed. With a cry, Maddy stumbled right, the wall shifting under her grasping hand, the doorframe sliding past her back.

"What's going on here?" shouted a voice. Suddenly, new hands grabbed Maddy and hauled her back over the threshold and out into the hall. Just as suddenly, Rory and his buddies turned on their heels and took off, leaving Maddy gasping against the wall.

"Thanks," she whispered. Breath shoved in and out; her heart thundered. Gradually, it quieted, and air came easier. Maddy looked up.

"Hey," said August. "You okay?"

Maddy nodded.

"I was in the art room, and I came out and saw those guys," August said. "What's with them? You know them?"

"Not really," said Maddy.

"They were trying to pull you into the guys' can!" said August. "We should go report it."

Maddy took a step back. Go to the office over a shoving match? It wasn't *that* big a deal, compared to…. Fear shifted through her, muttering warnings. If she reported this, Rory and his friends would get into trouble. They might come after her for it, like Ken, Robbie, and Pete. Or they might somehow tell Ken, and The Masked Avengers themselves would come after her. The possibility sent Maddy's gut oozing down her legs. She'd had enough of Ken and Co., and guys like them. Why couldn't they just leave her alone?

Leave me alone, she thought. *I just want everyone to leave me alone.*

"Maddy," said August. Her hand touched Maddy's shoulder. Startled, Maddy glanced at the other girl's face, away, then back again. August kept meeting her gaze, her dark eyes steady, her expression…*strong*, Maddy realized. August's face was strong, steady, and concerned, and not going anywhere. No, she looked ready to stand there and wait until Maddy found the strength somewhere inside herself to do what she needed to do.

And Maddy wanted that strength. Suddenly, more than anything, she wanted the strength to wear a face like August was now wearing. She wanted to *be* like August…and Kara…even her Trucker sister Leanne – part of the normal, functioning, don't-mess-with-me world again. But being part of that world meant taking on the bad as well as the good. Could she do it? Did wanting the strength mean she actually had it?

"Will you come with me?" she asked.

"You bet I will!" said August, a grin cutting across her face.

Together, they went to the office. A vice principal, Mr. Vaughn, heard them out. Admittedly, August did most of the talking, describing what she'd seen, and filling in words for Maddy when she hesitated.

"You were actually *inside* the boys' washroom?" asked Mr. Vaughn, observing Maddy. "The boys pulled you over the threshold?"

Maddy blanched. In her mind, the boys' hands were on her again, and then they started to change to other hands, and it was night, and…. Hunching forward in her chair, she hugged herself, breathing and breathing as she pushed against the memories, willing them back *down down down* inside herself.

"Maddy," a voice said quietly. It was August, her hand once again resting on Maddy's shoulder.

"Yeah," said Maddy. "I'm okay now." Straightening, she glanced at Vice Principal Vaughn, then away. "They had me... inside the washroom, sir," she said, her voice trembling. "And August pulled me back out."

"Okay," said Mr. Vaughn. "Did anything else happen? Do you need to see the school nurse?"

"No!" cried Maddy, ducking her head. "I'm fine!" A vice principal was one thing, the school nurse quite another. Next, it would be a psychiatrist.

"Let me get the boys' names," Mr. Vaughn said hastily. He took down the three names – August was able to supply the other two – and thanked them for coming in. "We have a zero tolerance policy for this kind of behavior," he added. "I may have to talk to you again, after speaking with the boys. Thank you for reporting this."

The girls left the office and stood a moment in the now-empty hall. Maddy knew she should head home – she was on supper prep – but something kept her lingering. August, too, seemed reluctant to go.

"Maddy," she said, her dark eyes flicking across Maddy's, "I don't know if I should say this. I've...heard some of the things kids are saying."

Maddy flushed. Shame seared her; she started to turn away.

August touched her arm. "It's not true," she blurted. "I *know* that."

Maddy hesitated. "*How* d'you know?" she asked, staring at the floor.

"I know you a bit," said August. "No *way* are you like that. I don't think anyone's like that, to be honest. It's just dirt talking – dirt that likes feeling dirty. That dirt don't have nuthin' to do with you."

The heavy weight pressing down on Maddy lifted slightly. "I don't know what to do about it," she said. "I get so many comments. And tweets. My Twitter is going private."

"My username is LivingSkyBrain," said August.

Maddy could picture it immediately – the entire sky filling the inside of August's head. "Mine's Yummibreakfast, with an *i*," she said with a small smile.

August giggled. "Well, you'll be hearing from me, Yummibreakfast with an *i*. Make sure you approve LivingSkyBrain."

"LivingSkyBrain will be approved," said Maddy.

"And, hey," added August, "don't think I didn't notice you got skipped for *The Pain Eater*. Did you want to be?"

"When it happened, I did," Maddy admitted. "Now, I don't know."

"Well," said August, "I'm the last one. You let me know, after Sheng does her chapter. If you want to have your say, I'll make mine end so it needs another chapter. Then I'll announce to Ms. Mousumi and the entire class that Ms. Yummibreakfast still gots to take her turn!"

The weight pressing on Maddy had almost vanished. "You serious?" she asked.

"You want the last word on *The Pain Eater*, you got it," promised August.

The thought made Maddy giddy. "Has Julie talked to you about it yet?" she asked.

"To influence me, you mean?" asked August. "Not yet. When she does, me'n her'll have an interesting conversation, don't you think?"

She and Maddy grinned at each other.

"And," August added, as if the thought had just occurred to her, "Julie and Ken Soong started going out about a week ago. She was talking about it in History, and I saw them smooching at the 7-Eleven. He's up next, right?"

"Yup," said Maddy, suddenly breathless.

"We'll see what *they* come up with together," August said drily. "Well, see you tomorrow, Yummibreakfast."

"Add me tonight," Maddy replied, turning toward the exit.

"Yummi tonight," called August as she headed the opposite way down the hall. "You got it."

• • •

The boy watching from the edge of the clearing was finished. The tension in him was obvious, Maddy thought – he was looking into the copse, but his body was turned away, as if he wanted to run. Just looking at him, she could feel her own body tense, and hear the blood pound in her ears. But nothing further – there was no sense of any memory about to rise up from within herself and take over, to pull her out of reality and into itself.

Cautiously, she began to sketch the outlines of the boys in the clearing. Two standing, here and here. A third on his knees, arms leaned out and down. The fourth…. No, first there was the fifth figure, the central one – the one everything else revolved around. The one who opened the door onto terror and pain. The pain eater. Tears stung Maddy's eyes. Yes, the figure at the center of this mural was a pain eater, she realized. An eater of other people's pain and fear. An eater of their violence and hatred. And an eater of silence – theirs and her own. An eater of poisons, none of them good.

How was she to draw this? How was she to communicate all of this in the shape of the face, the eyes? The color of the eyes? *Yellow*, she decided. *And the mouth.* Both should be brilliant with fear, what could not be spoken. The rest of the body would be shadow, a held-down form; all of the emotion had to go into the face. Tentatively, as if the chalk she held was high voltage, Maddy began to draw the face – her own face, the *feeling* of her own face. Not trying to make it better, not trying to make it brave and strong. Just terror, raw and screaming. Her own terror, right here under her fingertips. Her fingertips now drawing fear out of herself like pus out of a wound – saying, *Here it is. Here is what happened. Here is the me that was. She is me, I am going to let her be me. Me.*

Maddy had no idea of how much time passed. She was simply a body reduced to a direct line, the flow of the inner to the outer, onto the tree house wall. When she was done, two more figures had been completed: the girl on the ground, and the guy on top of her. Ken Soong, not that anyone could have identified him. But she knew who it was – she, Maddy Malone. She had drawn his crime here on her tree house wall, and now it was more than memory and silence. Now it could be seen, pointed to, defined. The drawing of the other three boys would have to wait; she was exhausted, trembling. Enough, already, for one Thursday evening's work.

But she was ready for him. Tomorrow afternoon, when Ken stood to read his chapter, Maddy Malone would be prepared.

chapter fifteen

Ken Soong got to his feet, accompanied by low cheers from his surrounding seatmates. His expression was confident; as he reached the front of the room, he nodded to Ms. Mousumi, who smiled in reply. Ken was active on the wrestling and swim teams, as well as in lunch-hour intramurals. Last year, he'd been a member of the Athletic Council.

He was popular, where Maddy went unnoticed. He liked an audience, where she shrank from one. A week ago, just glancing in his direction would have made Maddy feel as if she was going up in flames. Today, as Ken came to a halt and switched on his tablet, she felt shaky. Her breath shoved in and out; sweat broke out across her skin. When she forced herself to look directly at Ken, focus in on his grinning profile, her heart shouted in alarm and her body tensed, ready to flee. But she made herself stay with it – her gaze repeatedly jumping off but coming back, each time staying longer as her hands gripped the sides of her desktop, white-knuckled but helping her stay put. Because Maddy was here to listen – to hear every word, to watch every flicker in Ken's expression. In spite of his overwhelming advantage, she knew something he did not: that whatever he said today, whatever new slur or attack he was about to launch on the pain eater's already slaughtered reputation, she, Maddy Malone, would get the last word on it. And if she wanted to give her *best* last word, she knew she had to hear Ken's every syllable today. *Quiet*, Maddy told the blood pounding in her ears. *Shhhh, play stupid, play dead.*

Fingers touched her right hand. "Are you all right?" whispered Kara.

Maddy tried not to flinch obviously. She nodded.

About to start, Ken sent his gaze roving across the class, stopping just short of Maddy's desk. "We all know what kind of girl Farang is," he began. "She steals. She sneaks around at night and spies on people. She parties and..." – he smirked – "gets around. In all this time, name me one good thing she's done. She knows everyone's secrets, but does she try to help anyone? Instead of sneaking around, stealing and wrecking things, why doesn't she do something positive? But no, she hangs out with the partiers and gets pregnant. She had a choice. She didn't have to steal and drink and get pregnant.

"The boy thinks about these things. It's true he saw the priestesses almost drown Farang. And he felt sorry for her and brought her food. But then he keeps watching her. And he sees the way she really is.

"What he sees is that she asks for what she gets. She's lazy. She just hangs around all day, waiting for her free food. And after she gets it, she goes off and works on her suntan. She doesn't work in the fields and help with the harvest. She doesn't help collect herbs for the village healer. She doesn't help the old people. She could think about helping out and doing things for other people, but all she thinks about is herself. That, and getting drunk with the partiers. There's only one reason a girl like Farang goes to a party. She knows what she's getting into.

"So the boy gets to know Farang by watching her. And what he sees *disgusts* him. At first he felt sorry for Farang, but not anymore. No, Farang isn't the type you feel sorry for. But he has to be sure. So one day, he breaks the rules and talks to Farang. He follows her into the woods, and when he's sure no one else is near, he says, 'Hello, Farang.'

"She sees him there. She knows they're alone. What does she do? She comes on to him. The boy is shocked. He doesn't want this. But Farang won't stop. There's only one thing on her mind, and she's out to get it. 'Stop!' says the boy. 'I just want to talk to you.' But she won't stop. She knows what she's doing, all right. Soon the boy can't stop himself, because that's what boys are wired for. Besides, Farang *made* him do it. And so what happens? Farang gets pregnant again.

"So this is what I mean. Farang had a choice here. She could've talked to the boy and something could've come out of it. Maybe something big, maybe just a small thing. But something positive. The boy wanted to pull her out of the gutter, but she pulled him into the gutter instead. You've got to watch out for girls like Farang, keep yourself clean of them. The boy learned this the hard way. When the tribe found out what he'd done, they kicked him out. He was sent off into the woods to die. And it was all Farang's fault. They didn't kill *her*, because she was their pain eater and they needed her. They didn't need the boy. No one needed the boy, except maybe himself. I wonder what he was thinking while he lay there in the forest, starving to death. All because he wanted to help Farang. He died for Farang in the end. And she didn't even care. She was as bad as he was good. Too bad the boy didn't notice until it was too late."

As Ken paused, then shut off his tablet, Maddy felt the full weight of knowing descend upon her. So this was how he was presenting what had happened to other people. This was how he was describing the gang rape – as something *she'd* initiated, group sex *she'd* wanted because she was "that type of girl." It was all something she was "asking for," probably begging for. And the four boys? she wondered. Were the three rapists and their accomplice in his version all shocked innocents who ended up giving in to their "wiring"?

Her gaze darted over to David. Flushed, he was sitting with his eyes downcast, his face twitching. His lips twisted as if he was muttering aloud to himself, as if he was spitting out words. Not once did he glance up at Ken, and when Julie touched his arm and whispered to him, he jerked.

"Well, Ken," said Ms. Mousumi, getting to her feet. "Thank you. You may sit down." Her tone was cool, and she looked decidedly unimpressed. Ken got her drift. As he headed back to his seat, his grin had shrunk considerably.

"Any comments?" asked the teacher.

The class sat, musing. A hand went up. "I never thought about it – that she could've been doing something positive," said Harvir. "If you want people to do good to you, you gotta do something good for them."

"But she couldn't talk to anyone!" protested Theresa.

"And they all spat on her!" added August. "Once a month. You're complaining about *her* attitude?"

"Maybe," said Brent. "But after a while, she would've gotten used to it. I think Ken's right – she should've helped out somewhere. And when you think about what we all wrote, no matter whether you're for her or against her, no one in this class has written about Farang doing a single good thing for anyone.

"Well," he added uncomfortably, "maybe she saved the tribe from Zombiedom. But that was just to get a wish from the wizard, so it doesn't really count."

Again, the class fell silent. Ms. Mousumi waited them out, letting them think. Maddy sat as still as everyone else, her gaze darting hit-and-run-style across David. When Ken had sat down in his desk, David had leaned in the opposite direction, as if blown by a gale-force wind. Minutes passed, and he didn't straighten up. Ken kept glancing at him, obviously uncomfortable.

Kara's hand went up. "So maybe it did go like Ken said," she commented briskly. "Maybe Farang *did* get pregnant on purpose a second time. But maybe she had a reason for it. A baby would be company. At least *then* she'd have someone to talk to all day."

Without raising his hand, Ken shot back, "Why didn't she talk to the boy, then? She had her chance there, and she didn't use it."

Eyebrows lifted at his tone. Kara smiled slightly. "Looks to me like she and the boy talked just fine," she drawled in reply.

Snickers rippled across the class. "Okay," said Ms. Mousumi. She looked as if she'd heard all of *The Pain Eater* she wanted to for a while. "I have a comment that I'd like to make here. I want to disagree with your comment, Ken, that 'that's what boys are wired for.' Boys are not machines. They make choices with their minds, and their minds decide what their bodies will do – not the other way around. So they are responsible for all their choices, unlike a machine, which is not. I also think it's disrespectful to boys to think of them as being machines. They are human beings and should be *honored* as such, as should each and every girl."

The silence that followed Ms. Mousumi's short speech vibrated with intensity. No one looked at anyone else. Again, Ms. Mousumi waited out the silence, letting students struggle with their individual thoughts. Then she added, "We'll leave it there for today. Sheng, you're up Monday."

Seated at the center of the front row, Sheng Yoo nodded. Slowly, finger by finger, Maddy relaxed her death grip on her desktop. Her hands ached; her heart was performing martial arts; she had to keep swallowing the bile that surged up her throat. But she knew now. Through the tweets she'd received, comments from other students, and, finally, Ken's chapter, the situation had become overwhelmingly clear – Maddy now understood what other kids, August excepted, thought and said to each other when they looked at her. Nothing Ms. Mousumi said could change that; nothing any adult said ever changed the jungle of teenagers' thinking. Whether they were wired for it or not, once they got going they were all hunters looking for prey, and that was what she, Maddy Malone, was to them now – prey.

The question was where things were headed from here.

• • •

She made it out of the school building by shutting down inside, hunching in between her shoulders and keeping her eyes on her feet. If anyone spoke to her, she did her best not to notice. On one side of her locker, Tim Bing protected her from comments; he was the kind of guy who was immune to scum – just walked around handing out his cheerful smile to anyone and everyone. If he'd heard anything, he didn't let on, but Maddy wasn't in a grateful mood. Grabbing what she needed from her locker, she headed for the nearest exit. Once outside, she bolted down the sidewalk, skirting loiterers, but she wasn't fast enough to block out one last, shouted comment: "Maddy! Hey, *Maddy!* Let me be the father of your child!"

Four blocks from school, she was swarmed. It happened while she was crossing a small park – three boys jumped up from a bench where they were having a smoke and surrounded her, their voices jeering, their hands reaching. All three were

187

in grade nine; Maddy didn't know any of their names. "No!" she cried, crossing her arms over her chest, and the boys' hands shifted, going low. She doubled over to protect her groin, and they began pinching her butt, then punching it.

"What, you don't want us?" they leered. "But you like anyone you can get – that's what we heard."

Maddy was on her knees now, her arms over her head, the boys circling as if waiting. She felt it – that they were waiting for something – but what that something was, and whether they expected it to come from her or from them, she didn't know.

Abruptly, there came the sound of pounding feet and a shout, and then a figure launched itself at the circling boys. "You shits!" Maddy heard someone cry. "I'm not letting this happen again! Leave her alone! Get out of here!"

A few protests, some insults in reply, and the three boys scattered, disappearing into the late afternoon. Still, Maddy hunched, her arms over her head. Her heart kickboxed her chest; she sucked and sucked and *sucked* for air.

"Are you okay?" asked a voice. It was familiar. Lowering her arms, Maddy glanced up into David Janklow's face.

He reached out a hand. She took it, and he helped her rise. Hugging herself, Maddy continued to suck air.

"Let's sit down," said David. She followed him over to the bench. They sat as he waited for her to steady her breathing.

"How did you know?" she asked finally.

He was silent a moment. "I've been watching you for a while," he admitted. "I wanted to talk, but not at school. I didn't know if you'd…" His voice trailed off.

"What about?" she asked, her eyes on the ground.

He swallowed so intensely, she could hear it. "I'm sorry!" he exploded. "I'm just so goddamn sorry!"

"You didn't do it," said Maddy.

"No," David said bitterly. "I didn't do anything, did I?"

Maddy sat, silent. The moment was huge, too big to hold on to. She didn't know what to do with it.

"I couldn't believe what was happening," David continued, faltering. "It wasn't planned, nothing like that. We were just walking home from the play, and we saw you ahead. And then…they just all took off in a group. At first I didn't know what they were after. I ran after them. When I saw…I, like, froze. It was like I turned into concrete. I couldn't move." He was crying; Maddy could hear the gasp in his voice. But she couldn't look at him or respond in any way. Inside herself, the memory was starting to take shape. It was rising, about to come at her. Fighting – Maddy was fighting to keep it under control, to beat it back down, to kill it.

"My brother," said David, his voice breaking. "Keith. I couldn't believe *Keith*."

"D'you have a cigarette?" asked Maddy.

"I don't smoke," said David.

Maddy panicked. The memory was looming large – larger than David's words, the park, anything she could fix on. When it got this big, only burning would keep it at bay, and she didn't have that here. Sliding off the bench, she landed on her hands and knees. There was the ground – she could feel it, warmed by the afternoon sun. Maddy pressed her palms against it and the ground pressed back, solid, bigger than herself, bigger than anything that had happened or could ever happen. Sudden rage erupted in her. Lifting her hands, she began pounding them against the grass.

"Maddy?" said David.

She was grunting, snarling. And the sound wouldn't let up. Wordless, it kept heaving out of Maddy's mouth – sounds she'd never made before, sounds she'd never heard anyone make. Her fists pounded; her mouth snarled and spat; in her mind, she reached for the memory, and grabbed and tore and shredded it. As she did, the memory began to retreat. Gradually, the voices in her mind quieted; the grabbing hands shrank, then slid back down to wherever they lived when they weren't destroying her life.

Exhausted, Maddy lay down and let nothingness pour through her. No, not nothingness, she realized – relief. And then, slowly, triumph. She'd done it. She'd taken that monster memory into her own hands and defeated it.

"Maddy?" said David.

"You still here?" asked Maddy.

"Yeah," said David.

"Why?" asked Maddy.

David hesitated. "I'm not *them*," he said. "Not everyone's like *them*."

Maddy breathed a while. "What *are* you like, then?" she asked.

"That's the question, isn't it?" said David. "I didn't have the guts then. Do I now?"

Maddy sat up. "You got rid of those guys just now," she said.

"That's nuthin'," David muttered. "Nuthin' compared to ratting on my brother."

Maddy's mouth twisted. She gave him a sideways glance. "I don't know about you and your brother," she said. "I don't give a shit about your goddamn brother. That's your problem, and I'm not eating your pain."

Clambering to her feet, she headed across the park, a silent David behind her.

• • •

Saturday night, Maddy sat, chin on knees, observing the mural. It was finished. She knew this with a completeness of heart, a quietly enormous feeling of satisfaction that lapped at her like an inner ocean. She had brought the monster out of herself and trapped it in all its terrifying detail on the tree house wall. Which meant that in some way it was gone from her – gone from where it had lived inside her skin, inside her spirit. She wasn't free of the fact that it had happened – she would never be free of that – but it would no longer be happening *inside* herself, over and over. It was in the past now, and *she* was in the present.

The figures of the three remaining boys had been filled in. One of them, David's older brother Keith, stood with his head back, howling. Robbie held the central figure – herself – down by the shoulders, while Ken raped her. Pete prowled. At the edge of the clearing, David stood, frozen with shock.

The boys' masks hung, five pale leers, from the bare

branches of trees. The mural didn't display the boys' individual features clearly, but still Maddy had decided to unmask them, to tear off their plastic grins and throw them to the skies. Above all five, dangling from the highest branch, hung a single weeping mask, its truth. It was the last thing she'd drawn, the last detail she'd needed to add to the scene.

She couldn't believe she was done. The mural felt like a long black sickness that had lifted out of her; she'd thought it would be never-ending, and now it *had* ended. It was an enemy, and at the same time it had been part of her – part of her strength, her fierce seeking to overcome. And so, contradictory as it might seem, the mural had finally become a friend.

A sound outside the tree house alerted her. "Maddy," called a voice.

It wasn't Leanne – Trucker was at an out-of-town weekend volleyball tournament. Maddy crawled to the entrance. "C'mon up," she said.

Feet clambered up the ladder, and August's beaming face poked over the threshold, followed by Kara's. "Cool digs!" said August, clambering into the tree house. "This thing is stable, right? We're not all gonna keel over and tumble to the ground? Whaaaa—?"

Her eyes hit the mural and she fell silent. Beside her, Kara came to a halt, also stock-still as she studied the image. Wordless, Maddy knelt, watching Kara's face. She respected August – knew how her own energy and self-esteem doubled in the other girl's presence – but here before the mural, it was Kara's reaction she was waiting for, hoping for, seeking.

"This happened to you," said Kara. Her voice was hoarse, guttural. She spoke without looking at Maddy, her gaze riveted.

"Yes," said Maddy.

Kara continued to crouch, motionless. "It's like a scream," she said. "A black scream."

"Yes," whispered Maddy.

"I wish," said Kara, blinking rapidly, "my brother could've screamed like this."

Maddy remained silent; there was nothing to say to something like that.

"What's that?" asked August, pointing to the cream-gold sphere Maddy had drawn midair. "It's not the moon – that's over there."

"I don't know exactly what it is," said Maddy. "I drew it after the background, but before anything else. It just had to be there."

"Okay," said August. "What are those?" She pointed to the masks.

"Comedy masks," said Maddy. "From *Our Town*, when they gave them out to the audience. Were you there?"

"No," said August, "but I heard about it. Is that when it happened?"

Maddy hesitated. Even after the mural's completion, even after inviting both girls over specifically to show it to them, she felt shaky. "After," she blurted out. "Coming home. They jumped me in a bunch of trees. They were wearing the masks."

"Do you know who they were?" asked Kara.

"Yes," said Maddy. "I figured it out. One I knew then, the rest later."

"Who?" asked Kara and August, their voices overlapping.

Maddy stared into their eyes, the shocked intensity of their gaze. The necessary words felt enormous, like tombstones leaving her mouth. They would change everything; she knew this. Nothing would be the same ever again.

"Ken Soong," she said. "Pete Gwirtzman. Keith Janklow."

August let out a whoosh of air. "David!" she said. "*That's* why!"

"He was there," said Maddy. "He didn't do anything. He's the one at the edge of the trees."

"He didn't help?" demanded Kara.

"He told me he froze," said Maddy. "We talked yesterday. I don't think he could've stopped them anyway."

"That's not an excuse!" protested August. "He should've done something!"

"Something like that happened to me once," said Maddy. "A teacher was picking on one of my friends." She described the incidents with Mr. Zarro and Jennifer Ebinger, then added, "I froze then too. I was right there and I could've said something, but I didn't. Not because I didn't *want* to. It was like something invisible was holding me back."

"It's not the same," said August, shaking her head.

"Nothing's the same," said Maddy. "But I know what David meant. It's something that just *happens* to you."

Silence swallowed the tree house. The three girls crouched staring at the mural, the only sound their hoarse breathing. Maddy didn't know what to say next, what the soul words were. She'd called these girls on her phone earlier that afternoon, told them how to find the tree house, and invited them over for eight p.m. Now she was at their mercy. She waited.

"Who's the guy holding you down?" asked August.

"Robbie Nabigon," said Maddy. "That's all he did. He didn't actually...rape me."

"Have you told anyone?" asked Kara. "Your parents?"

"Not yet," said Maddy. "I wanted to finish this first. I had to."

"Yeah," said August. "If I had something like that hanging around *my* gut, I'd want to get it out too. It's like the end of the world."

"And the beginning," said Maddy.

For the first time since entering the tree house, Kara looked directly at Maddy. She was crying slightly; the smile she gave Maddy was lopsided. "Maddy," she said, "you're a fucking incredible artist."

Maddy gave her a lopsided smile back. "So you believe me?" she asked, her voice cracking.

"Believe you!" exploded August. "We *heard* Ken's chapter! *And* David's."

Maddy sagged like a collapsed balloon. "Okay," she whispered, the word barely audible. "Okay."

"Did you think we wouldn't?" August asked incredulously. "After all the rumors going around school? What're we – blind and stupid?"

"I didn't mean that!" protested Maddy.

"Maddy," said August, crawling close and poking her face directly into Maddy's, "I believe you. Absolutely. Period."

Maddy stared into the dark eyes inches from her own. Tears slid down her face. "I didn't know," she quavered, "how you'd be. This is the first time this has happened to me."

"I believe you too," Kara blurted, touching her arm. "All those times with your hands in class. Now I know why."

Maddy rubbed her sleeve across her eyes. "Sorry I'm crying," she mumbled. "I'll try and stop."

"You cry as long as you want," said August. "It's a free country."

And so the three of them sat quietly while Maddy sobbed out her relief. It had been so long – the aloneness, the silence – and now it was over. She'd guessed, she'd taken a risk, and she'd chosen wisely. These were two friends who would stick by her.

"Want to go into the house for ice cream?" she asked. "But don't say anything to my parents – about the mural, or what happened. I'll tell them soon. It's just – this is enough for tonight."

They climbed down the ladder and went into the house.

chapter sixteen

Monday morning before classes, as Maddy was standing at her locker, Pete Gwirtzman walked past, wearing a Greek comedy mask. August, who was standing next to Maddy, let loose an incredulous hiss.

"I don't believe it!" she muttered. Then, glancing at Maddy, she added, "Oh yes, I do! Who was that? Could you tell?"

"Pete," said Maddy, shaky and at the same time exhilarated that someone else had seen – she now had some kind of evidence. "They've done stuff with masks before."

"That sticker!" August exclaimed. "The one that was on your binder!"

Maddy nodded. "They sent me a mask tweet too, and called themselves The Masked Avengers."

August glared down the hallway at Pete's receding back. "Well, they're about to meet The Pissed-Off Avengers!" she snapped. "Last night I wrote my chapter for *The Pain Eater*. I'm going to ask Ms. Mousumi if I can read it today, after Sheng reads hers. Then I'll announce you're doing the last chapter. We'll show them who they *can't* push around!"

"But you haven't heard Sheng's chapter yet," protested Maddy, stunned by the quantum leap forward that August wanted to make. "How could you know what to write?"

"I didn't really have to," August shrugged. "What I wrote will work no matter what Sheng wrote. But just to make sure, I called her yesterday and we talked about it. She'd already written her chapter, Saturday afternoon. She didn't tell me exactly what was in it, but I did manage to get enough out of her."

Maddy was stuck somewhere between the urge to flee and further exhilaration. "But aren't you're supposed to wait to write your chapter until *after* the person before you reads theirs?" she asked.

"Actually," said August, waggling her eyebrows, "Ms. Mousumi never said that *specifically*. Besides, my dad says I'm a real charmer. I will just have to summon up all my powers and work them upon her." Abruptly, her excitement left her, and she focused in on Maddy with concern. "You do still *want* to write the last chapter, don't you?" she asked. "You look kind of pale – like you're about to hit the floor."

"I just don't see how it's going to work," Maddy mumbled, shutting her locker door and leaning her forehead against it. Her stomach felt as if it was swimming laps through her gut. Life had been difficult enough dealing with The Masked Avengers – trying to foresee their next move, to keep, at all times, out of their collective sight. Now here was August, moving in and taking over in a way Maddy could never have predicted.

"We'll talk about it at lunch in the caf," said August, giving her an encouraging pat on the arm. "I won't do anything without your say-so, okay? Kara'll be there too."

"Okay," agreed Maddy. "Only I might be a bit late – I've got something I have to do first."

"Not *too* late," said August, turning to head off down the hall. "Or I'll come looking for you."

The start of the lunch hour found Maddy hesitating outside the art room door. Her head was down; inside her mind, she was stepping toward the doorway then away, then toward it again. What she wanted to do here felt enormous, bigger than what her thoughts could hold. She'd never done anything like it before; there was no way to foresee how it would turn out. Furthermore, it was hers to do on her own. August and Kara would have readily agreed to come with her – Maddy knew this – but this moment belonged to her, and her alone.

A rush of students came at her, and Maddy stepped through the open doorway to avoid them. Ahead of her the room was empty, except for a single figure at the back, who appeared to be going over paper supplies.

"Excuse me," Maddy faltered. "Mr. Zarro?"

The teacher turned toward her, and a smile took over his face. "Maddy!" he exclaimed. "Where have you been? We've missed you this year."

Maddy swallowed and started toward him. "I guess I wanted to talk to you about that, sir," she said.

"Okay." Mr. Zarro set down the stack of paper he was holding and stood, obviously in listening mode.

"Well," said Maddy. She paused. Her face felt flushed and her heart had started a deep, dull thud. Mr. Zarro was watching her with such a warm, expectant expression. What she was about to say would change that. Maybe she should skip the ugly stuff and pretend she'd come in for a different reason. But sometime soon, she was going to have to speak uglier, more difficult truths. If she couldn't be honest here, how would she manage later on?

"I wanted to tell you why I didn't take art this year," she said.

"Okay, shoot," said Mr. Zarro.

"Do you remember Jennifer Ebinger?" asked Maddy.

Mr. Zarro frowned, the friendliness vanishing from his face. Fear washed over Maddy and she took a step back; she fought the urge to turn and run.

"Jenn sat beside me in grade nine art," she said, her voice wobbling.

Mr. Zarro maintained his frown. "Yee-es," he said.

"Well," said Maddy. She rested a hand on a nearby counter for support. "I thought you weren't...fair to her, sir."

Mr. Zarro's gaze dropped, and he studied the floor. He cleared his throat. "I don't see that this is any of your business, Maddy," he said. "But if Jennifer wasn't happy with her final mark—"

"I don't know what her final mark was," Maddy broke in hoarsely. "I never saw any of the marks you gave her. But I did see her crying in class a couple of times over things you said to her. Maybe she isn't Rembrandt, but all she wanted to do was draw, sir. I don't think the way you treated her was right."

Mr. Zarro rubbed a hand over his face. A bright flush was creeping up his neck. Maddy's heart went into overdrive. For a moment, she did almost turn and run.

"And that's why you didn't take art this year?" asked Mr. Zarro after a long pause, his gaze still fixed on the floor.

"Yes, sir," said Maddy.

"And, I suppose," said Mr. Zarro, after another long pause, "that's why Jennifer didn't take grade ten art either."

"I don't know why she didn't take art this year," said Maddy. "We've never talked about any of this."

"You haven't?" asked Mr. Zarro, his eyebrows rising.

"No, sir," said Maddy.

The teacher took a deep breath and shifted his gaze to the classroom window. "Well," he said. "I'm sorry…this has happened. That wasn't my intention. Sometimes I can be…harsh."

"Sometimes," said Maddy. "But you can also be really great, sir."

Mr. Zarro's eyes reddened. He blinked rapidly. "And here you are, missing art because of…." He shook his head. "One of my best students. And one of my bravest." With a forced smile, the teacher held out his right hand. Confused, Maddy stared at it.

"I want to shake your hand, Maddy," Mr. Zarro said quietly.

"Oh!" said Maddy. Quickly, she took his hand and they shook. A bit giddy, she giggled.

"Thank you," said Mr. Zarro. "I'm glad you came and talked to me. It's too late now to do anything about art class for you this year, but I've just started an after-school club for students interested in learning about stained glass. It's normally only for grade eleven and twelve students, but I'll make an exception for you if you're interested."

"Stained glass!" cried Maddy. "I'd love to!"

"Then I will see you Thursday afternoon, directly after last class," said Mr. Zarro. "And Maddy – if you happen to see Jennifer, could you ask her to come see me sometime soon? I'd like to talk to her."

"She's in my French class," said Maddy, turning to leave. "I'll for sure tell her, Mr. Zarro. Thanks!"

Mr. Zarro didn't respond. But when Maddy reached the doorway and looked back, the teacher was watching her. Without speaking, he raised his right hand and saluted her. Maddy waved back, and headed to the cafeteria to meet August and Kara.

• • •

That afternoon, Maddy walked into English class buffered by August on one side and Kara on the other. The sensation was a little like being inside a mobile fortress; to her surprise, Maddy realized this was the first time all semester that she wasn't entering a classroom alone. Beyond her two friends, she could feel the class watching, their eyes speculative and distant – as if she was a character in a movie. For reasons out of her control, she had been lifted out of her regular, mundane life and become something for others to observe, to obsess over, to judge – all without bothering to talk to her, to get her side of the story. As if there was no other side, as if she had no story to tell.

When the three of them reached Maddy's desk, August hung around, putting on a show of casual chitchat. Maddy giggled at all the right places – giggled on hyperdrive, in fact, her laughter loud and forced – but she found it hard to concentrate on the conversation. Every time she glanced up, she caught kids flashing her glances. Something new seemed to have hold of them – something edgy, something that was making *them* nervous. In the back row opposite, Nikki, Sean, and Elliot were huddled over a phone, and they kept looking from it straight at Maddy, then back again. All three were smirking as if they'd borrowed Julie's face, and as Maddy watched, her heart sank. Nikki had a mean streak – she knew that from personal experience – and no one needed personal experience to know what Sean and Elliot could dish out. Whatever was on that phone screen would blow Maddy's mind, she was sure of it. Who did she think she was kidding? Her future was over and no one could save her – not August, not Kara, not anyone.

"Okay, this is it," said August in a low voice. "I am now going into high gear." Squaring her shoulders, she crossed the short distance to Ms. Mousumi's desk. As Maddy and Kara watched, she flashed the teacher her most brilliant, persuasive smile, and began to talk. Ms. Mousumi listened, frowned slightly, listened some more; then, to Maddy's astonishment, the teacher began to nod. Leaning back in her chair, she said something to August. August nodded quickly, obviously agreeing to some kind of condition, and returned to Maddy's desk.

"It's a go!" she hissed, before proceeding toward her seat. "She said to listen to Sheng's chapter, and if mine follows it okay, I can read it today. Then it'll be you on Wednesday!"

"Did you tell her about me missing my chapter?" Maddy asked in confusion, but August was already out of earshot, passing Paul and sitting down to his right.

Ms. Mousumi stood to call the class to order. As she did, Maddy glanced at the back row by the door. There was Ken, talking to Harvir to his right. To his left, David – no, Maddy realized with shock, David's seat was empty. Was he skipping again? Were things getting so hot with Ken that he couldn't face coming to English anymore? Then she spotted David sitting three seats over from his usual desk, in a formerly empty one between Harvir and Elliot. At that moment, Julie slid over one seat, into David's former desk, bringing Dana and Christine one seat over with her. Ken turned to them with a grin, and he and Julie began snuggling. If Ms. Mousumi noticed any of this, she didn't comment. But she hadn't commented on David's Leaning Tower of Pisa act either, Maddy reflected. Perhaps she was simply relieved David had solved his obvious conflict with Ken without outright hostility.

Sheng Yoo stood and approached the front of the class, carrying a tablet. Slender, with long hair and glasses, she had a reputation for being studious and conscientious. Maddy had once heard her say she intended to be a lawyer. Coming to a halt, Sheng switched on her tablet. She sent her gaze once across the class. If she made direct eye contact with Julie, Maddy didn't notice.

"It was almost the full moon," Sheng began, her voice clear and even. "In another month, Farang would turn sixteen. She sat by her secret altar, thinking about her life. She had no friends. She didn't even know who her parents were. The only people who would talk to her were the partiers, but they were rough and cruel. Farang didn't want to get pregnant again. She'd lost two babies – that was enough.

"She was so, so lonely. Her whole life was a waste, just pain and more pain. And as far as Farang could see, there was one person to blame for it all: the high priestess. The other night, when Farang was spying, she overheard the priestesses talking. That was when she learned they planned to kill her. Soon after her birthday – they didn't say the exact day. So now Farang knew her life was never going to get better. In fact, it was about to get a whole lot worse.

"She decided she had nothing to lose. She snuck into the temple to where the knives were kept. These knives were used for sacrifices and were very sharp. Farang chose a small one that she could carry inside her sleeve. Then she snuck into the room where the priestesses slept.

"The high priestess slept closest to the door, probably so she could sneak out at night without waking up the others. But this was also a help to Farang. She crawled to the high priestess's pallet and knelt there, watching her sleep. The high priestess wasn't all that old – maybe in her thirties. In her sleep, she looked normal, not evil – like somebody's mother, maybe yours or mine. But Farang knew better. She knew the high priestess was nobody's mother and never would be. The high priestess was the priestess of death, and now she was going to die.

"Farang raised the knife and brought it down. But the high priestess was too quick. She shapeshifted into a python. Before Farang knew it, the python wrapped around her hand that was holding the knife and squeezed. So she dropped the knife. Then the python shot up around her throat and squeezed there.

"Farang's life passed before her eyes. She knew it was ending. She let out a cry and the other priestesses woke up. Because of the kulumulu necklace, everyone knew about the high priestess's shapeshifting, so they weren't too surprised. But with the other priestesses watching, the high priestess couldn't kill Farang. Farang was the tribe's pain eater, so she was special. She couldn't die until the gods decreed it, and it had to be done exactly right at a special ceremony.

"So the high priestess let Farang go and shapeshifted back to human. And in that second, Farang got her chance. She snatched up the knife and stabbed the high priestess. The high priestess fell to the floor dead, and Farang ran from the temple into the forest.

"She had defeated her enemy, and she was still alive. But the question was what to do now. And this was where Farang turned back into the loser she was deep in her own heart. She didn't change. She didn't say, 'Enough is enough!' and leave the tribe. No, the next morning she was at the temple, waiting for her free food again. A priestess brought it out to her. They had to feed the pain eater – that was the law. They knew it and Farang knew it.

"But one thing *had* changed – the high priestess was dead. Farang hoped this meant she wouldn't be killed, she could keep on living and being the tribe's pain eater. But she didn't think of changing her life beyond that. Whether she believed in being the pain eater or not, she didn't try to change it. She didn't leave. And so, in the end, I have to say I don't feel sorry for her. I'm not saying she asked for it, just that she didn't ask for anything. Farang was a nothing, a zero. A non-life. She may as well not have been born.

"That's the end of my chapter." With a flourish, Sheng shut off her tablet. She glanced expectantly at Ms. Mousumi.

The teacher shifted in her seat. "I have a question for you, Sheng," she said. "Farang is a character that *you* created. *You* decided who she would be and what she would do. So it's actually *you* who decided she wouldn't leave the tribe and try to change her life. Why did *you* make that choice?"

Confusion twisted Sheng's face. "I didn't create Farang," she protested. "The rest of the class did. I was just following *their* ideas. That's what I was supposed to do, wasn't I?"

"But in your chapter, *you* chose not to make her leave," said Ms. Mousumi.

"Because she didn't *before*," said Sheng. "Even after everything that happened, she didn't leave *before*. So I didn't think she would now."

Ms. Mousumi nodded. "What does everyone else think?" she asked.

As Sheng returned to her seat, Julie's hand went up. "Sheng's right," she declared. "Why would Farang leave now, if she never did before?"

Theresa's hand shot up. "Two reasons," she said. "She knows they're going to kill her – number one. And, number two, *she* just killed someone."

Unexpectedly, Sean's hand went up. "But she *is* a loser," he said. "She takes everything they dish out. Maybe she actually *likes* it, and that's why she sticks around."

"Good poisons," Elliot drawled beside him.

"Doo doo doo doo," Brent sang softly from across the room.

"That's enough," Ms. Mousumi cut in sharply. "You will speak respectfully, or not at all."

A dense silence fell on the class. For a long moment, no one spoke. Sean smirked at Nikki, who raised a cool eyebrow in reply. Then David raised his hand.

"I think maybe it's easier to think Farang is a loser," he said slowly.

Ms. Mousumi's face quickened with interest. "Why do you say that?" she asked.

"Because then that's *all* she is," said David. "You don't have to think about *her* anymore. You don't have to think about how she's hurting. How she's lonely. How everything was taken away from her. How maybe *you* could help to change things for her." He shrugged. "It's just easier."

"Maybe it's easier for *her*, too," Ken shot back, leaning forward in his seat to look around Harvir. "She's that way because she *wants* to be that way. If she *wanted* to be different, she wouldn't have been *there*."

Maddy's eyes widened. Beside her, Kara gasped. Four desks over, August cleared her throat.

"Been *where*, Ken?" she asked hoarsely.

Ken turned to glare at her, his face slamming closed. "The village!" he snapped. "Of course! I meant the village in the story – what else would I mean? Farang should've left the village and headed out on her own, like Sheng said."

Kara's hand went up. "And maybe wear a smiling, happy mask when she killed the high priestess, so no one would know who she was?" she asked.

Whoa! thought Maddy. Suddenly, things were moving fast – faster than her heart was beating. Across the room, Ken's gaze darted between herself, Kara, and August.

"Okay," said Ms. Mousumi, her gaze taking the direction Ken's had taken, then returning to him. "Some interesting points have been raised here. Does Farang leave or doesn't she? Is she the shaper of her own destiny, or does she simply accept what happens to her? The final answer is about to be given by August Zire, who has told me that she's ready today with her chapter. How about it, August – are you ready to finish this off for us?"

"I am," said August, her voice rock-solid determined.

"Why don't you come up here, then?" said Ms. Mousumi.

As August got to her feet, Ken gave her a level glare. Two seats over, David stared down at his desktop. And hunched in her front corner desk, Maddy Malone sat silently counting heartbeats.

chapter seventeen

August walked purposefully to the front of the room. As she passed behind Kara and Maddy, she ran a finger along their backs – a secret gesture, a promise between her and them. Kara had started this story, and now August and Maddy were finishing it. With everything that had been written in between – soul stones, The Beautiful Land, good poisons, and *she asked for it* – in the end, the meaning of it all came down to the three of them. And they were ready to deliver.

August came to a halt at the front of the class. She studied her first few lines. Lifting her head, she glanced around the room, making sure she looked directly at Ken and Julie. She smiled. "It was the day before the full moon," she began. "Farang's sixteenth birthday. There was no party for her, of course. Everyone ignored her as usual. That night, they were going to spit their pain onto her the way they always did – that was the only present she'd get. Except that now there'd be no poison in her food. Since the high priestess's death, no one poisoned Farang's food. She was still getting the tribe's pain, which did hurt her, but no poison. So she was growing stronger inside herself. Y'see, poison keeps you weak and sickly. Now that Farang wasn't getting the poison anymore, she was strong and healthy. This made her very different. For years, she was always weak. Finally, it was starting to feel good to be alive.

"The morning of her birthday, some people rode into the village. They came from the capital city of the kingdom of Faraway. This was a long way off, and where the high priestess got her PhD in Evil. At the head of this group was a woman – the high priestess for the main temple in all the land. They went to the temple in the village and met with the priestesses. The villagers were curious. Hardly anyone came to their village, ever.

"That night, everyone gathered together. Things went as usual. Farang waited in the bushes while the people danced and sang. Then she crawled out and they spat their pain onto her. But Farang was now so strong and healthy, she barely batted an eye. She crawled into the cage and ate the food. Then she lay down and relaxed. The people danced faster and faster, but Farang just lay there, enjoying herself. Because she was healthy, their pain was no longer a big deal. The villagers couldn't do much to her anymore, and she knew it.

"The high priestess from the capital city watched and was impressed. There were rumors about a village pain eater of great power, and she was here looking for her. This pain eater was predicted in the ancient holy books, and a special star was now showing up in the night sky. So the high priestess stood up and stopped the dancing. She called Farang out of the cage and bade her kneel before her.

"'Farang, you were to die in three months' time,' the high priestess told her, 'but I have come to offer you a great destiny. Instead of dying, you will come with me to the capital city of Faraway. Because the king needs a new pain eater. The king's pain eater has to be better than all the others. There are special pains for this pain eater to eat. But the king's pain eater lives differently from other pain eaters. You will have a lovely apartment in the castle. Fine clothes and food will be brought to you. Servants will bow as you pass. For you will be the king's pain eater, and know all his secret woes. Once a month you will suffer, and it will be terrible. But the rest of the month will be a life of luxury and ease. Everyone will envy you.'

"The villagers whispered in excitement. They couldn't believe this was happening to Farang, *their* pain eater. Such an honor for the village! The high priestess had to raise a hand to quiet them.

"'I await your answer, Farang,' she said. 'Will you be the king's pain eater?'"

August paused. The class sat silent, their gaze fixed on her. Maddy sat with the rest, the blood thudding in her ears. Whatever August had Farang choose, Maddy would have to follow up on it. She darted a sideways glance at Kara, who was watching August with an approving half-smile on her lips.

August lowered the pages she was holding, and turned to face Ms. Mousumi. "That's the end of my chapter," she announced. "But it's not the end of *The Pain Eater*. There's still one more chapter, and that one belongs to Maddy Malone because she got skipped two weeks ago, when it was her turn."

A look of surprise crossed Ms. Mousumi's face. "Is this true, Maddy?" she asked, turning to look at Maddy.

Maddy felt the eyes of the entire class descend upon her. "Yes," she managed.

"How did I miss you?" asked Ms. Mousumi.

"You weren't here," said August. "A substitute teacher was here for three classes, because you were sick."

"Oh yes," said Ms. Mousumi, her expression clearing. "Well, then—"

Ken's hand shot up. "This isn't fair," he said briskly. "Maddy should've said something back then, if she wanted to. *We* all had to follow in order."

"Oh, I don't think that matters," said Ms. Mousumi. "Everyone gets a turn – that's the point of the exercise."

Julie's hand went up. "But the story was going a certain way," she protested. "Now Maddy'll step in and change it."

Ms. Mousumi's eyebrows rose. "Of course, she'll change it," she said. "Just like you had a chance to change it, and everyone else."

"But they *knew*," Ken broke in. "Maddy and August – they've known for two weeks. Why didn't they say something sooner? Because *they* wanted to take over the story for *themselves*, and end it *their* way. Not really fair, I don't think."

Ms. Mousumi frowned. She glanced again at August, then at Maddy. "Is this true, Maddy?" she asked. "Have you and

August been conspiring for two weeks to take over the story and end it your way?"

Maddy grimaced, groping for the right words. "No," she blurted. "It just...happened that way. I mean, I knew I got skipped, but I didn't say anything at first because..." She paused, losing out to the flush that had taken over her face. "It just happened," she repeated lamely. "I was upset, I guess, about...other things, and I didn't say anything."

The teacher's gaze softened, and she nodded. "We all have those kinds of days," she said warmly. "And I'm actually the one at fault, for not noticing. I don't think Maddy should be penalized for my error. And, personally, I would love to hear Maddy's contribution to *The Pain Eater*. So the class will be hearing from you, Ms. Maddy Malone, two days from now on Wednesday. Okay?"

At the front of the class, August broke into a brilliant grin. Beside Maddy, Kara whistled softly.

"Okay," said Maddy, her heart exploding in her chest.

"All right then, August," said Ms. Mousumi. "Thank you, and you may sit down. We've got a lot to do today, and since this wasn't the final chapter, I think we'll reserve class comments until Wednesday. Now, if you'll all open your books to..."

August rounded the back of the teacher's desk and came up behind Maddy and Kara, en route to her own desk. Lifting the pages she had curled in her right hand, she bopped Maddy gently on the head.

"It's all yours now, Maddy," she whispered, and walked to her seat.

• • •

One hour later found Maddy and Kara sitting on bright orange stacking chairs outside Vice Principal Vaughn's office. August hadn't been able to join them due to a dental appointment, but Kara had been filled in on all the pertinent details, and was wearing a determined, don't-mess-with-me expression. It made her look remarkably like August. Maddy wasn't sure if this made her feel nervous or possible. Her growing friendship with these two girls was changing so many things. Was she ready for all of it? Did it make any difference if she was ready?

"This man is a lot more popular than he looks," muttered Kara, twisting a loose strand of her long brown hair around one finger. "Come on, Mr. Vaughn – we've got life waiting for us sometime this century."

The door to Mr. Vaughn's office opened. "You can go in now, girls," said a secretary, nodding at them.

They stepped into the office. With a smile, the vice principal closed the door and sat down behind his desk. "Take a seat, ladies," he said. "What can I do for you?"

Kara sat down, then leaned forward. "We're here because we'd like to know what's happening with that assault on Maddy," she said. "When those guys tried to pull her into the can. It happened last week – five whole days ago."

"Yes, I remember," said Mr. Vaughn. "Well, Maddy, I spoke with all three of them, and we reviewed the footage from the security camera posted in that area of the hall. Some of the incident was recorded, though most of it was at an angle the camera doesn't catch."

"And?" prodded Kara.

Mr. Vaughn cleared his throat. "The boys say it was a harmless prank, a spur-of-the-moment thing," he said. "They weren't intending anything by it. They've apologized and served some detention time."

A frown crossed Kara's face. "They didn't apologize to Maddy," she said.

Mr. Vaughn's eyebrows rose slightly. Steepling his fingers, he tapped them together. "You're right," he said. "I overlooked that, and I apologize. It's a bit late in the process now, but I can set up a meeting for an apology from the boys if you'd like, Maddy."

Maddy watched his fingertips tap together. She thought of the three boys, the contempt that had twisted their faces. *Come over to my house to play. Come over to my house to fuck, Mad Maddy.* Any apology from those guys would be a mere formality – it wouldn't mean a thing. Mr. Vaughn knew it, and Maddy knew it. But she understood why Kara was pushing for it.

"Did you call their parents?" Kara asked.

Mr. Vaughn nodded. "Parents are routinely notified in cases like these," he said.

"Mine weren't," blurted Maddy. Her voice came out hoarse, an explosion in her throat.

Mr. Vaughn looked surprised. "I'll double-check on that," he said. "It *is* policy. They should have been."

"Well, they weren't," Maddy said.

Mr. Vaughn wrote something down on a notepad. "I'll get to that right away," he said.

Maddy ran her gaze over him – the expressionless face, the natty striped tie, the once-again steepled hands. Dislike engulfed her. She sat up straighter. "They're lying, Mr. Vaughn," she said gruffly. "They wanted to get me in there and rape me. I know, because it's happened to me before – rape. It happens a lot, you know. It would've happened then if August hadn't rescued me."

Mr. Vaughn's eyebrows rose again. "None of us know what *might* have happened," he said. "And I can't punish the boys for something they didn't do. But I will certainly bring them in to apologize to you, if that's what you would like."

Maddy took a long, raw breath. "I don't know if that's what I'd *like*," she said. "But yeah, that's what I *want*." As Kara swelled with pride beside her, Maddy leaned forward in her chair, strengthening her focus on Mr. Vaughn's face, intensifying it. "Because this is serious, Mr. Vaughn," she continued. "I'm not a bump on a log, I'm a person. I'm important. And I deserve an apology, whether they mean it or not."

Mr. Vaughn observed her silently.

Whether you *mean it or not*, Maddy added in her head. She got to her feet. "Don't you have to go babysit your neighbor's kids?" she said to Kara.

They left Mr. Vaughn's office without saying anything further to him, then stood in the empty hall outside the main office door, thinking over what had taken place. "He wasn't even going to get them to apologize to you!" Kara fumed. "He was just going to ignore you, like you weren't hardly even involved. But you told him, Maddy! You told him just fine!"

"Yeah?" asked Maddy, glancing at her.

"Yeah," said Kara, her voice punching the air. She took a deep breath. "And I have something for you. Just a sec." Sliding her knapsack off her back, she rooted around in it and pulled out a single piece of paper. "I wrote this for you last night. It's a poem. *Not* a masterpiece, so don't expect Shakespeare. Here."

"This is for me?" asked Maddy, surprise welling up through her as she accepted the piece of paper. White with blue lines, it was a regular piece of foolscap. Still floating in astonishment, Maddy read the hand-printed words:

A Poem for Maddy Malone

Now sky is my sky.
I feel the sun rise up my throat.
I speak starshine, moon wonder, flying meteors.
Until the end of the world,
I am here to begin.

Warmth washed Maddy's face. She blinked swiftly. "That's *way* better than Shakespeare," she said. "Thank you."

"I was sitting on my bed after doing homework and I got to thinking," Kara told her softly. "About how when things get really crappy, it can feel like you're over. There's no chance for a change, something better to happen. Like with Frank." Her voice trembled and she stopped, staring at the floor. "I guess sometimes it really is like that. But not always. Not with you, Maddy. Okay?"

Their gaze locked, and Maddy saw that Kara was teary-eyed too. "Okay," she whispered.

"Okay," Kara said again, and they were quiet a moment. "Well," she sighed, "I have to go babysit. Will you be okay walking home on your own?"

"Yeah," Maddy assured her. "Kids'll be home by now. No one'll be hanging around."

Kara nodded. "See you tomorrow, then," she said.

A smile opened suddenly in Maddy, flashing up from her toes. "Yeah, see you tomorrow," she said. "And thanks again for the poem. I love it."

They parted, and headed out of the school into their separate lives.

• • •

Maddy walked into her bedroom after supper dishes to find her sister sprawled across her bed, examining Maddy's phone.

"What're you doing with my phone?" Maddy blurted, too shocked to be angry. "And how come you're in my room?"

"I'm reading your mentions," Leanne replied without looking up.

"No, you're not!" cried Maddy, lunging at her, but Leanne slid the phone under her butt and lay on her back, simply looking at her.

"What're you gonna do?" she asked. "Go tell Mom and Dad?"

Maddy backed off. There was no way she could take on her jock sister in physical combat and win. And Leanne had obviously read enough of her mentions to know Maddy couldn't complain to their parents. Or could, but for some unfathomable reason, was choosing not to.

"How'd you get my password?" asked Maddy, crossing her arms.

"Just watched you," said Leanne. "You might as well display it on a billboard, you're that obvious."

Maddy flushed. "Okay, so what'd you find out?" she mumbled. For a while now, she'd been blocking most of the accounts tweeting at her – if tweets didn't come from family or a close friend, she no longer saw them. But she couldn't do anything about new accounts in her mentions. She'd stopped checking her notifications – hadn't opened that tab in days.

Leanne's expression was unreadable. "Half the school seems to think the other half of the school has fucked you," she said. "Multiple times."

Maddy's flush deepened. "Oh, *that*," she said. "That's old, Trucker. Very, *very* old."

Leanne observed her silently. Then, as Maddy watched, her sister's face softened. "Come on, Maddikins," she whispered. "We're not enemies. I'm on your side. I always was."

Maddy's face twisted and she fought off the urge to cry. "Since birth," she conceded.

"Conception," said Leanne. "Come here."

Crawling onto the bed, Maddy lay down beside her sister and let Leanne put an arm around her. "It took me a while to catch on," said Leanne. "I was mad at you for shutting me out, so I unfollowed you. I knew something was going on, but because I was mad at you…" Her voice trailed off. "Well, I was hurt, I guess. I heard some things – just mean stuff, nothing like this – but I ignored it. Kids wouldn't say the worst things around me, I guess. Then, at the tournament this weekend, I heard some more…stuff I couldn't *believe* I was hearing. But Sunday night when I got home, the homework I had to catch up on was *crazy*. And I was pretty sure if I asked you straight out, you wouldn't tell me what was going on, because if it was happening to me, *I* wouldn't be talking, either. So I decided, first chance I got, I'd check your phone."

Leanne's arm tightened convulsively. "Maddy, that stuff is garbage. Sewer thinking. You're *not* psycho, and you're *not* the world's least choosy slut. You're my little sister, same as you always were, and I want to know why this is happening to you."

Maddy stared up at the ceiling. Enveloped in her sister's warmth, in the coconut scent of her hair, she wanted to give in, to surrender to the closeness that had always connected them, at least until the last half year. At the same time, something inside her resisted – something that pushed back; something that locked tight into itself.

"And that gives you the right to steal my phone and invade my privacy?" she demanded, stalling for time.

"Yup." Leanne's voice revealed not the slightest twinge of remorse.

"I don't *think* so," said Maddy.

"If you don't tell me now, I'm going to take your phone and show it to our beloved parents," said Leanne.

Maddy's heart started its deepest, most painful thud, battering her from the inside out. "I talked to Mr. Zarro," she blurted. "Today. He let me join an after-school club for stained-glass making."

"Cool," said Leanne. "Two minutes, Maddy. Then I'm going to Mom and Dad."

"Wednesday," Maddy bargained. "Just give me 'til Wednesday after school, and then I'll tell – you *and* Mom and Dad."

Wednesday was the day she was due to give the closing chapter of *The Pain Eater*, and Maddy *had* to contribute the last word on Farang's destiny on her own – without helpful, well-meaning interference from her sister, her parents, and whatever would come out of telling them about the gang rape. Because if she told them, something *would* come out of it – something definite and immediate. And she needed more time – two more days – to work out Farang's story, her own story, and how the two intertwined, by herself.

"Why Wednesday?" asked Leanne.

"I'll tell you *on* Wednesday," said Maddy. "After school. I'll walk home with you."

"I have a game," said Leanne. "A home game."

"I'll come to the game," said Maddy. "We'll walk home after."

"No way – you're actually coming to one of my games?" said Leanne.

"Sorry," said Maddy. "I'll come to every single one from now on."

Leanne lay silently, considering. "That new mural you're working on in the tree house – does it have anything to do with this?" she asked.

Maddy stiffened. "Did you look at it?" she asked.

"Not since the first time," said Leanne. "Too creepy. Thought I'd check your phone first."

"There's a reason for the creepiness," said Maddy. "Wednesday, you'll know why."

Leanne pondered further. "Well, you *have* been better this past week," she admitted. "But I still don't like it. Kids are saying ugly, *ugly* things about you, Maddy. I want to know why."

"Wednesday," repeated Maddy. "Promise. Cross my heart, hope to die."

Leanne let out a whoosh of air. "Okay," she said. "But you're eating lunch with me tomorrow. *And* you're walking to school with me in the morning. That'll be early – I've got practice."

Maddy groaned. She could just see it – plodding alongside her sister while Leanne laid out the entire day for her: when they were going to meet up, what Maddy should do and say when harassed. Two full days of being broadsided by her sister's love…. Well, it was better than being ignored. And she would bet her last dollar that none of The Masked Avengers would dare to even glance her way while Leanne was within punching distance. There were advantages to having a senior jock sister nicknamed Trucker, bossy or otherwise.

Maddy surrendered. "Okay," she said. "I'll come watch your morning practice tomorrow. To make up for the games I missed. Pax?"

"Pax," said Leanne.

chapter eighteen

The following morning, Maddy escorted her sister to school. She sat on the gym sidelines, bleary-eyed, as the senior girls' volleyball team ran laps and spiked balls. She even managed not to scream when, at a signal from Leanne, the entire team came at her, hoisted her onto their shoulders and carried her around the gym, singing "For She's a Jolly Good Fellow!" When they set her down, Maddy was giddy with giggles, convulsing with them. The team crowded around her, patting her back and cheering her name. The air shimmered with goodwill.

"Okay, ladies," called a beaming Coach Wurzer. "Showers for everyone or you're gonna stink up your classes."

The team headed for the changeroom, still cheering Maddy's name. Watching them go, Maddy wondered how much Leanne had told them – not that she cared, really. Whatever it was, the team was certainly on her side. Not everyone thought she was the world's least choosy slut, and just knowing that, *feeling* how much the team had wanted to show their support… well, it put a decidedly different slant on things. The comments that came at her later that morning still hurt, but they no longer staggered her heartbeat. Maddy started working on her shrug response.

Still, things were edgy in a way she couldn't quite catch hold of. Like Nikki, Sean, and Elliot in yesterday's English class, it was all quick glances, hit-and-run sneers, students looking at their phones then at her with eyes that knew something she did not. Then, in her morning math class, an image of a naked woman hanging from a guillotine was sketched onto the whiteboard when the teacher momentarily stepped out. And Maddy was tripped in the hall as she was heading to her French class, her books scattering as she hit the floor. No one extended a hand to help her up; no one even slowed to look. But the worst came in French, where Jennifer Ebinger sat one desk ahead, her back rigid, her silence loaded.

Jennifer's refusal to speak to her left Maddy feeling as if she'd been sucker-punched. What had happened with Jenn? she kept wondering. Maddy hadn't talked to her about Mr. Zarro yet, so it couldn't be that. Had Jenn heard one of the rumors going around? Had she read something online? *Had she believed it?* What was it that moved in on kids and ate their minds like this? Tired out by thinking about it, *aching* from it, Maddy headed to the nearest girls' washroom at lunch break. She pushed open the outer door and made for the farthest cubicle of three, which appeared to be the only empty one. As she reached it, the cubicle door nearest the washroom entrance opened, and Julie came out.

Maddy froze. Still in the process of doing up her jeans zipper, Julie looked up and their eyes met. Julie's eyebrows rose, and she gave her signature smirk.

"Hello, Maddy," she said.

Maddy didn't know why it was – graphic hallway comments didn't bother her anywhere near the way that smirk did.

"Mad mad *mad*-for-it Maddy," Julie added in a singsong.

The middle cubicle door opened and Dana emerged. When she saw Maddy, she snorted. "Smut slut," she quipped, crossing to the counter and depositing her books. "What I haven't read about her on Twitter ain't worth mentioning."

A flush seared Maddy's face. Heat invaded her brain; all rational thought went up in smoke.

"I heard she was at Stan Sassoon's party last week," said Julie, crossing to the counter to stand beside Dana. "And she gave it up free of charge to whoever wanted it."

"Does she usually charge?" asked Dana.

"They even gave her a bedroom all to herself," sniggered Julie. "*And* whoever dropped in to see her, of course."

Dense with shock, Maddy could barely move. "I wasn't at any party," she blurted.

"Not what I heard," cooed Julie, turning to examine her makeup in the mirror.

"Definitely not what I heard either," said Dana, winking at Julie.

Maddy stared at the backs turned to her, the reflection of

the two smirking faces that watched in the mirror. Watched the way kids watched all day long – sideways in their desks, sneering over their lunches, and tossing endless comments as they passed in the halls. Gone was the memory of Leanne and the team; gone was the inner voice telling her to keep cool, to shut the hell up and get out of there. Inside her brain, heat swelled, fused into quantum thermodynamics, and exploded.

"I wasn't at any party fucking whoever came along!" she shouted. "I haven't been at a party in months – *seven* months. You know why? You know why the goddamn hell why?" Raising a hand, Maddy pointed it at the now-wary faces watching her in the mirror. "Because *your* boyfriend and two of his friends raped me last March. Yes, *your* boyfriend," she screamed at Julie. "Ken Soong. Pete Gwirtzman. And Keith Janklow. All of them together. And it was *rape*, not sex. They weren't *my* boyfriends – *I* didn't want them. So *fuck* you and your goddamn lies. Now you know the truth. Eat *that* and see how you like it."

Julie turned around, her face pale, her eyes intense. For a moment, she simply stared at Maddy. Then her head tilted back slightly, and her eyes glazed over. "I don't believe that," she said airily. "I just don't believe it." Turning again to the mirror, she began fiddling with an earring.

Incredulous, Maddy stared at the two girls. Without speaking to each other, they were focused intently on makeup and fashion accessories. Dana gave a little cough; Julie sighed.

"What d'you think today's lunch special is?" asked Julie.

Her eyes were still glazed, her expression almost dreamy. *The Beautiful Land*, Maddy thought, watching her. *That's where she is.* If it had ever occurred to her to wonder how Julie had come up with the idea, she had her answer now. Crossing to the washroom entrance, she got the hell out of there.

• • •

Lunch with Leanne, Kara, and August was stressed. Maddy told them about her washroom encounter with Julie and Dana. The three girls responded with indignation and encouragement. They were everything Maddy needed, the exact best kind of sister and friends anyone could ask for in a situation like this. But she felt guilty for putting them through what they were facing for her – as if all the ugliness were somehow *her* fault. And she kept thinking about Jennifer's silent back, the way the other girl had refused to speak to her. Maddy knew she could count on Leanne, but Kara and August – would that silence someday take them over the way it had Jenn?

English was a repeat of the day before. David again sat between Elliot and an uncomfortable-looking Harvir; his face grim, David didn't seem to be talking to anyone. Julie and Ken openly snuggled; watching them, Maddy wondered if Julie had told Ken what had happened earlier in the washroom. No, not possible, she decided. Not with the way they were cooing at each other.

"Pigeon brains," was Kara's comment as she observed them. "Pigeon *shit* has a higher IQ."

Everyone watched Maddy. Not outright – the glances came at her like light dancing off a mirror ball, moments of eyes flicking across her face and gone. It was almost as if the class were on a collective joyride at her expense: the more miserable she felt, the more excited their smirks became. But not everyone had joined in. Here and there, a pair of eyes watched her steadily, the face thoughtful – Rhonda, Theresa, even Harvir. A few students seemed oblivious; incredibly, they appeared not to have tuned in. But tuned in or not, they were all waiting… waiting for Wednesday and the last chapter, Maddy's final word on the fate of Farang.

"You're ready to go with your chapter tomorrow?" Ms. Mousumi asked, coming over to Maddy's desk with a questioning smile.

Maddy nodded. She didn't trust herself to speak. Beside her, Kara spoke up for her.

"Maddy'll do a great job," she said firmly.

"I'm sure she will," Ms. Mousumi said, but she was eyeing Maddy uncertainly. "Maddy, I'm just wondering…is everything okay with you?"

Maddy stared down at her desk, a flush creeping up her face. Thumbnail welts were once again wedged in across the back of her left hand. *One more day*, she thought, suddenly exhausted. One more day and it would all come out – the end of Farang's story, and the end of her own. At least, that was the way it felt. How could life go on after what she was going to have to tell her family? Was she strong enough to handle it, or would the experience destroy her – shred her like a used Kleenex?

Under Maddy's desk, Kara's left hand settled onto Maddy's right one and squeezed. It was enough to allow Maddy to get a grip.

"I'm okay," she said, glancing sideways at the teacher. "I'll have my chapter ready for tomorrow. Don't worry."

Ms. Mousumi hesitated. "Well," she said, "I'm looking forward to hearing it." And she walked to the front of the room to call the class to order.

• • •

That evening, Maddy sat in the tree house, the two flashlights trained on the mural and a notebook propped on her knees. It was chilly – she was wearing a jacket over a thick sweater – but she was about to start her chapter for *The Pain Eater*, and it had to be written here: she knew that if she knew anything. After school, she and Leanne had walked home together, and Maddy had told her sister the story of Farang, chapter by damning chapter. They had sat at the kitchen table over cups of hot chocolate as she'd described the last few chapters, and when she'd finished, Leanne had said, "That's not the story of Farang, Maddy. That's the story of your *class*. And *you* get to top it all off."

Top it off in more ways than one, Maddy thought now as her eyes traveled over the mural, taking in details of the trees, the masks, the six figures…the moon caught on a tree branch and the cream-gold sphere hovering in the background. That sphere was where it had all begun, where she'd started to put form and *knowing* to things. And yet it was almost formless, just a soundless, revolving glow. What was it? Maddy wondered as she observed the image for probably the thousandth time. Why had it called itself into being? What was its meaning?

Getting to her feet, she crossed to the mural and stood before the sphere. Inches from her forehead, it seemed to pulse with an inner radiance. That radiance was gentle, sweet, and oddly familiar. Riveted, Maddy stared at the sphere. Blood pounded in her ears; her heart started a dull, painful thud; a cry leapt from her mouth. Then, like a blossoming flower of light, the sphere seemed to open, and something passed from it directly into Maddy's forehead. She felt it like gentle fire, like angel wings, like the breath of a soul coming home. *Oh!* she thought, beginning to cry. *Oh my goodness!*

It was *her* goodness, her own good soul – the part of her that had left her during the rape because it wasn't able to bear what was happening. Now, finally, it had returned. Sitting down, Maddy hugged and rocked herself, welcoming the lost part of herself home.

• • •

Midway into Maddy's first paragraph, her phone rang. Picking it up, she hesitated, then asked, "Hello?"

"Maddy?" said a male voice. She recognized it, but couldn't place it.

"Yes?" she said.

"It's David. David Janklow," said the voice. "I got your number from Jennifer Ebinger."

"Oh," said Maddy. A sinking sensation came over her, as if she was draining into her feet. Together, she and David breathed through a pause.

"They want to talk to you," he blurted. "Tomorrow before school. It's about *The Pain Eater*, what you're gonna say."

"Why?" asked Maddy. "It doesn't have anything to do with them."

"So just tell them that," said David. "I think it'll be okay then. If you say that, it should be okay."

"You tell them," said Maddy.

"They want to talk to *you*," said David. "They won't hurt you. They're not gonna do anything. They just want to talk. 8:15 at the 7-Eleven, okay?"

Maddy was silent. Her heart thundered.

"Maddy?" said David. "Maddy? You there? Look, don't you think you've been getting better lately? It's not bothering you as much now – you're getting happier, more like you used to be. So don't you think maybe you could forget about it all? Since it's not really bothering you anymore, and you've gotten over it."

Maddy's voice, when she spoke, dragged against her throat. "Just another good poison, eh?" she said.

"No!" cried David. "That's not what I meant. But this afternoon Ken was talking about how maybe we could all be friends. They could make it up to you for what they did. This is about my *brother*, Maddy. Don't you think…" David paused, breathing raggedly, then took a deep breath. "Besides," he added, "you don't want to hang around with *August*, do you? Maybe you and Julie could—"

Maddy shut off her phone. Then she sat a while, doing her own ragged breathing. Whatever David's real intentions toward her were, his phone call made it clear he was under too much pressure to be of much help. Not that she'd expected any, but still…. Eyes closed, Maddy sat grimly fighting off waves of nausea. *One more day*, she thought. *Just one more day, and then what?*

Who knew, but she had a chapter to write. Picking up her notebook, Maddy reread what she'd written earlier. Then she looked at the mural and the cream-gold sphere. Everything seemed to be coming at her at once – inside herself, it felt as if everything that had happened since that fateful performance of *Our Town* last March had risen up and was swirling around like a hurricane. Well, it was time to let it out – to let the words decide for themselves what they wanted to be. Touching pen tip to paper, Maddy began to write.

• • •

Maddy heard the first sounds just as she was finishing up. She had written the last word, set down her notebook, and was staring at the mural when she heard a rustle of leaves in the backyard, then the quiet murmur of voices. Not the voices of her parents, or Leanne and her friends calling to one another – these were voices keeping themselves quiet, voices that didn't want to be heard by anyone but themselves. Straightening, Maddy sat a moment, following the progress of carefully placed feet around the side of the house. Whoever this was didn't seem to have looked upward, to have noticed the dim light that must be coming from the treehouse – for now, at least, she was safe. Picking up her phone, Maddy thumbed.

"Dad," she said to her father's hello. "There's someone in the backyard. Creeping around. I don't know who."

"Where are you?" asked her father.

"The tree house," she said.

"Stay there," he said and hung up.

A moment later, Maddy heard the house's back door open, followed by a sonic blast from what was probably Leanne's boombox, as the Red Hot Chili Peppers flattened the neighborhood. Then the yard lights came on, the boombox went silent, and Maddy peered down through the trap door entrance to see her father and Leanne stalking every inch of the now quiet backyard.

"Maddy!" called her father. "You okay?"

"Yeah," she called back. "Are they gone?"

"I think so," said Ian Malone, coming to the foot of the tree. "But someone *was* here. They knocked over the paint cans I left by the porch. You'd better come down."

"You come up first," said Maddy. "And bring Mom and Leanne. I want to show you something." Because she knew now. She knew now was the time: there was no more putting it off; what had to be done had to be done. Heart thundering, she repositioned the two flashlights and listened to her family climb the ladder. Her father's head rose through the entrance first, followed by her mother's. After they crawled in, their eyes took a moment to adjust to the light. Then Ian Malone absorbed his first glimpse of the mural and let out a groan.

"Maddy?" her mother asked faintly, her gaze darting across the image. Leanne, climbing in on their heels, remained silent, kneeling before the mural and memorizing every detail.

"When?" she asked finally, and then, "Who?"

Maddy began to speak, her mouth the opening onto a cave that went deep into herself. Each word was huge and dark, part of a truth that had lived long underground and was now rising upward, seeking light. She shook as she spoke; tears poured down her face; she had to keep wiping her nose on her sleeve. But the words knew themselves; they were ready to emerge. She trembled, but she did not falter. She told her family everything – date, names, the masks torn off.

They knew enough not to touch her until she'd finished. Even afterward, they sat a while apart, silently studying the mural. "What is this?" asked Leanne, pointing to the cream-gold sphere.

Maddy felt the wistful smile that slipped across her mouth. "That's The Beautiful Land," she said. "Where I went when it happened – where a *part* of me went. It was beautiful there. No bad things happened. The Beautiful Land took care of that part of me until it could come back.

"The rest of me that never left…well, this is what helped me here." Getting to her feet, Maddy undid her jeans and let them drop. Then she pointed to the burn scars that ravaged her inner thighs.

Her father sucked in sharply. Her mother moaned. "The bastards," Leanne whispered. "I'll kill every one of them."

"It helped me," Maddy said hoarsely. "I needed it for a while. I don't anymore."

"Thank god for that," said her father.

Maddy pulled up her jeans.

"I feel so badly that you couldn't tell us sooner," said her mother. "What did we do wrong? I'm sorry—"

"It's not your fault," Maddy assured her. "It was just too awful. Like a killer living inside me. It felt like I would die if I even *thought* about it."

"Oh, honey," said her mother. "Come here."

Maddy crawled into her mother's arms and stayed.

"Maddy," said her father. "A Mr. Vaughn called tonight, from your school. He told me about some boys who tried to push you into a washroom. Was that somehow connected to this?"

Maddy nodded. "Yes," she said. "Kids have been on my case about it. There's been other stuff too."

"Tell me about it," muttered Leanne.

Her father was silent a moment. "Well," he said slowly, "there seems to be so much we don't know about. I don't want to push you, but how are you now? I know it's tough, but the police..." His voice trailed off.

"The police didn't help Rehtaeh Parsons," said Maddy. "And I don't even have a photograph."

"We have to try, honey," said Ian Malone. "Those boys could do it again. To someone else. We'll be with you, every step of the way."

"Rehtaeh's family loved her, too," said Maddy.

Her mother hugged her tightly. "What happened to Rehtaeh was very, very sad. But we can't stay there, Maddy. We have to move forward. We have to believe change is possible."

"Yes," whispered Maddy. "I know it has to happen – the police and all that. But it's just…. It's going to be hard. I'm not sure…"

"Not sure what?" her father asked gently.

Maddy's face crumpled. "Not sure I'm strong enough," she said, breaking down again. "I want to be, but I don't know if I can."

Taking one of her hands, her father waited until her sobs quieted. "I think you're strong enough," he said. "I can see it in that mural you drew – incredible strength and courage. But when you need a little extra strength, Maddikins, we'll be here. Your mother, Leanne—"

"You got it!" interjected Leanne.

"And me," finished Ian Malone. "All of our strength together – for you. Okay?"

Maddy took a shuddery breath. "Okay," she breathed.

"How about we go now?" said her mother. "It's only 8:20. We'll set the security alarm, and then we'll all go together."

"First, let me get the Nikon to take some pictures of this mural for the police," said Mr. Malone. "It'll do a better job than my phone. That is, if it's okay with you, Maddy."

Maddy nodded. A half hour later, the entire family was on its way to the downtown police station.

chapter nineteen

Maddy got to her feet. The gaze of the class lay heavy upon her, a collage of expectation – the majority of it speculative, some openly hostile, and, here and there, moments of sympathy. As she took her first step, Kara touched her arm and whispered something, but Maddy was already in motion and didn't hear the words. Glancing at Ms. Mousumi, she saw the teacher smile encouragingly; as Maddy came to a halt at the front of the room, she had the urge to nod to Ms. Mousumi, then the class, and say, "Good afternoon, your Honor, ladies and gentlemen of the jury."

Out of the entire class, only she knew Leanne was out in the corridor, sitting with her back to the door, where she'd positioned herself once class had officially started. Leanne had initially wanted to bulldoze her way into the room, even stand beside Maddy as she read her chapter, but Maddy had insisted on shouting distance and Leanne had reluctantly agreed. After Maddy had given her victim statement the night before, the police had told her they would be assigning her case to an investigator in the next few days. That investigator would then contact her, and the case would proceed from there. Which meant that Ken didn't yet know she'd been to the police, and neither did David – Maddy hadn't even told Kara and August. After the comments they'd made to Ken following Sheng's chapter, she wasn't sure they'd be able to keep their mouths shut about her police report, and finishing Farang's story in front of the class felt like enough stress for one afternoon. Then, to complicate matters further, as she and Kara were coming down the corridor toward the English classroom, Jeremy had stopped them. His eyes hadn't quite met theirs, and his face had been twisted with distaste – not for Maddy, but for what he had to tell her. "Someone got onto the website," he'd blurted. "I think it happened last night. They must've hacked their way in. Farang's name's been changed to yours, Maddy – all the way through. And stuff's been added."

"What kind of stuff?" Kara had demanded.

Jeremy's eyes had shifted away, uneasy. "I don't want to say," he'd mumbled. "But I don't think Ms. Mousumi knows – at least, she's not acting like she does."

This was true – as the teacher had called Maddy to the front of the room, she'd given no sign of realizing what had taken place. About a third of the class also appeared unaware, but for the remaining two thirds, as well as for Maddy, the same process seemed to be coming to a conclusion: that of a gradual, seven-week merging of Maddy and Farang. In the minds of most of those watching her, Maddy thought, she and Farang were now one and the same – this was as true for Kara and August as it was for Ken and Julie. It was equally true for herself. For almost two months now, she and Farang had been approaching this moment, and Maddy felt the Faraway village girl waiting for her – waiting to be given her chance. In all the chapters that had preceded this moment, no one except Rhonda had allowed the pain eater to speak. Other than "I can and I will!" she hadn't yet said a single word.

From her seat in the back row, August gave her an enthusiastic double thumbs up. Kara looked expectant, openly curious. Julie's gaze was narrowed and predatory; beside her, Ken sat stonefaced, and David slumped in his seat next to Harvir, looking as if he was cultivating an ulcer. And then were all the others who'd invested in this story, pondering and hoping it along – Harvir with his soul stones; Paul, who no longer kicked dogs; Jeremy, who'd tried to touch the horror; Rhonda, with her "I can!" and Sheng with her lawyer's mind, asking, "Why doesn't she leave?" Maddy didn't have answers for all of their questions – she figured she'd probably missed most of the loose threads. In the end, all she had was herself, what *she* could bring to this story. That was going to have to be enough.

"The high priestess from the capital city stood looking at Farang," she began. "Farang of Faraway, who was kneeling before her, dressed in rags. Farang looked like a beggar, a nothing. But she was more than that – a lot more. Because the allura leaf poison had taught her to read minds, so she could hear what the high priestess was thinking. And in the high priestess's mind, Farang saw that if she went to the king's palace, she'd be fed more poison in her food, like the first high priestess did to her here. Only it'd be worse. There'd be a lot more poison. Sure, she'd have beautiful clothes and a nice place to live, but she'd have horrible suffering too. On top of that, she'd die in one year, because the king got a new pain eater every year. But of course they weren't telling her that. So the deal they were offering her was really just lies. The king and the high priestess and all their friends were liars. And anyway – how can you trust someone who wants you to suffer?

"So Farang said, 'Let me think it over tonight. I'll tell you tomorrow.' The high priestess said okay, and everyone went to bed. But Farang didn't sleep like the others. She snuck into the temple and the old high priestess's office, and stole the basket of soul stones. Then she went around the village and left the soul stones with the people they belonged to. In the morning, each villager woke to find their soul stone right beside them. There was great rejoicing. It was like after a very long hot summer, when everyone thinks and dreams about rain, and then finally a beautiful gentle rain comes – everything you long for falling through the air, down onto your skin and heart.

"The people all had their souls back. And so did Farang. That morning, she placed her soul stone on top of her secret altar and danced around it, singing. The whole altar was built in a beautiful shape that just waited for that soul stone, and the stone fit it perfectly. When Farang put her soul stone on top of her altar, she felt like she had everything she needed. *I can!* she thought. *I can!*

"She left the altar and walked into the village. The people stood with the high priestess from the city. Everyone waited for Farang. They didn't smile or cheer when they saw her. No one said thank you for the soul stones. They'd been taught to hate her for so long, it was a bad habit now. But they felt confused. For the first time, they were really thinking about Farang, their pain eater.

"Farang stood before them. She said, 'I've decided. I won't go to the city to be the king's pain eater. And I won't be the pain eater here anymore, either. I've given you back your souls, and now I'm giving you back your pain. Because souls and pain go together. Sure, there's happiness, too. But if you're alive, you're going to feel pain. Zombies don't feel pain. Bumps on a log don't feel it, either. But if you're truly alive, you do. You can't give your pain away, not really. What's yours is yours – that's just the way it is.

"'I'm not saying pain isn't hard.'" Here Maddy paused, thinking about Kara's brother Frank. This had been the most difficult part to write, and it was equally difficult to say it aloud now. She didn't look at Kara. "'Pain can be so scary, it can almost kill you,'" she said, her voice trembling. "'Sometimes it even can kill. But still, hurting someone else won't take away your hurt. It just adds more hurt to the world.'"

Maddy was crying now. The words she'd written out so carefully the night before blurred and ran together on the page. Closing her eyes, she continued to speak, reciting as best she could from memory. Because memory was on her side now; it was with her. "'We have to figure out a different way,'" she said. "'Because I'm not eating your pain anymore. And I'm not eating my silence anymore, either. Silence is a poison, and it's not a good poison. I'm sick of it and I'm spitting it out, all of it. D'you know none of you have ever talked to me? You don't know *anything* about me. So you don't know I taught myself to spin and weave. I know how to make weapons and hunt, and I keep a small garden where I grow my own food. I can take care of myself. I don't *need* you.

"'So *fuck* you and everything you wanted to do to me. What would you have done if this happened to you – if it happened to you *just because you were there?* I have a right to live, just like you do. I have a right to be happy like you, to have friends and hope. I can and I will! I am not going to be silent and secret and full of your hate anymore. No wonder you hate me – when you look at me, you see everything you did to me or thought about me. It's not *me* you hate, it's *yourself.* That's a problem *you* have to fix.'

"Then Farang turned and left the village. She didn't go far. She went a ways into the woods and began building a hut for herself. No, she didn't leave. She knew now there was no Beautiful Land anywhere else. Here was where she decided to stay. So that means the next part of the story is up to the villagers. Because the villagers are as big a part of this story as Farang. So far in this story, we've all been criticizing Farang – every move she makes, every breath she takes. But she isn't alone – she lives in a village full of people.

"What about the villagers and *their* choices? Every day, they make choices about Farang – *not* to help her, *not* to stick up for her…just to make her life worse and worse and *worse*. Is that because they lost their souls? Well, now they've got them back. What does that do for them? Do they smarten up, or do they kill Farang like they're supposed to in three months? Do they let Farang live, but leave her alone and without friends? This is a story about all of us – how we are together. It's so important, how we are together…"

Maddy's voice trailed off and she stood, eyes closed and alone in the great silence that followed her last words. It wasn't an exciting ending, she knew that. No blood-drooling zombies stumbled out of the forest. No kulumulu stones changed color. No one shapeshifted. The story basically ended where it had begun, except for the soul stones, which had been reclaimed. But who cared about soul stones in this day and age? Who cared about truth, and what really happened, especially if knowing the truth brought pain?

The silence stretched out, heartbeat after heartbeat – taut, excruciating. And then, finally, came the first sound: a slow, deliberate clapping. Startled, Maddy opened her eyes to see Harvir leaning back in his desk, his dark gaze steady on her as his hands came together, unhurried, almost leisurely, announcing his approval. A second later, from across the room, Kara joined in, followed by August, and Paul and Jeremy and Theresa. Ms. Mousumi got to her feet with a broad smile on her face, then Rhonda began to applaud, and Nikki. Not everyone followed suit – Ken continued to sit stonefaced, as did Julie and her retinue. David, too, remained motionless, staring at his desktop. Elliot gazed out the classroom windows; Sheng played with a pen.

Still, the heartbeat clapping continued on, and Maddy realized she would never forget the gift of it. If it didn't include everyone, it was enough. She had her soul back. Whatever was coming, whatever she was going to have to face, like Farang of Faraway, she knew she was now strong enough to walk toward it.

acknowledgments

The author gratefully acknowledges editor Stephanie Fysh's stellar contributions to the text, particularly in the area of the Internet and cell phone usage. Thanks also to Sargeant Dean Liebrecht of the Saskatoon Police Force, for his information concerning the filing of a sexual assault complaint. A third big thanks to Katherine Fellehner, grade nine student and the pride of Biggar, Saskatchewan, for the use of her gorgeous photograph on the cover. Thank you too to Fletcher Bumphrey and Doreen Chapman for their comments regarding plot and cover, and to Logan Sanderson for being such a source of inspiration. And, finally, a warm smile for Second Story Press – they are simply a privilege to work with.

about the author

BETH GOOBIE grew up in Guelph, Ontario. Beth moved to Winnipeg to attend university, became a youth residential treatment worker, and studied creative writing at the University of Alberta. She is the award-winning author of more than twenty books, mainly for young adults, including *Born Ugly*, *The Throne*, and the CLA award-winning *Before Wings*. Her first adult novel was *The First Principles of Dreaming*. Beth makes her home in Saskatoon.